A Decade of Misunderstanding

Ada Gardener

All rights reserved; no part of this publication may be reproduced or transmitted by any means, electronic, mechanical, photocopying or otherwise, without prior permission from the publisher.

First published in Great Britain in 2023. KDP publishing.

Copyright by intellectual property law 2023 Ada Gardener.

ISBN 9798857551448

Any similarity to persons living or dead is purely coincidental.

For everyone who has loved and lost. And for Liam…because I said I would.

Then an idea came to him. Picking up some small pebbles, he dropped them into the pitcher one by one. With each pebble the water rose a little higher until at last it was near enough so the crow could drink.

- From the tale of the Crow and the Pitcher

"Whilst focusing on the black dot, you forget the white square."

- Bill Rogers, *Effective Classroom Management*

"Be with me always - take any form - drive me mad! Only do not leave me in this abyss, where I cannot find you! Oh, God! it is unutterable! I can not live without my life! I can not live without my soul!"

- Emily Brontë, *Wuthering Heights*

Clara 2019

Waking once again, feeling like there is a hole in middle of her body, one you could just slide a hand right through, and a gripping, a fighting, something unpleasant that she doesn't have a name for yet. Get up, it's worse lying here, it is not real, you are a being, your mind is doing this to you, be present, it is not a thing, you have felt this way every day of your life but you just keep forgetting, you will forget tomorrow as well, get up, get on with the day - this is her new mantra.

She used to think everyone woke up feeling this way. That was before she knew about collective human experience, or repetition compulsion or that it is possible to wake up feeling one way every day for your whole life and not even realise it. Clara thought, most people don't feel this way: they feel calm, peaceful, excited, nothing at all.

She stared at the bedroom ceiling: it had a hair-line crack running from the side by the bay window to the white, cylindrical hanging light fitting. The house was always shifting very slightly.

We feel - and have no way of knowing what is real, true, projected, shared, imagined; it just is.

Clara's aunt Alice, the one who runs a multi-million pound office furniture company, told her once that the hardest part about getting out of bed is just putting your feet on the ground. There is some truth in it.

But some days the ground glides away.

Aunt Alice was a role model twenty years ago - round, motherly, determined, successful, really hilarious. Jovial. Kept her poetic husband in the manner to which he had become accustomed - writing in his poet's shed at the bottom of a project garden (her project - landscape design degree on the side), long suffering his over-indulgence and flirtations. It was a comfort when Alice put an arm around Clara when she was 21 and said about the putting of the feet on the ground. It meant that she had felt it too - or something like it.

This same aunt has a tumour now. Clara had thought, when she found out, god the infallible are fallible and success has no meaning.

Clara puts her feet on the ground. And walks. It is September; the light comes through the 1930s stained glass window at the top of the staircase. It casts the pink and the blue onto the floorboards on the landing.

Bathroom: the toilet seat is up and there are Lego bricks in the bath. Clara thinks if she wasn't here, the bath would become the permanent Lego brick container and the toilet seats would just be removed like they are in those back street toilets in other countries where no-one bothered to buy the seat as well as the bowl.

There are usually twenty minutes in the morning when no one else is up. And usually this is filled with breakfast TV and the blissful subduing of catastrophic world events - it is incredible training, the way in which they can make global disaster, the end of humanity and the utter incompetency of those governing the country seem to fit so seamlessly with a story about a sensational goal and a priceless painting of the beheading of John the Baptist found in someone's loft and how they smile right through it all, japing and jollying all the while. It's good to know they have been up since 3am - did they get the same feeling as Clara this morning - they remind her of the brave face, the lipstick face, the face-the-music face, the professional face. The daytime hours adopted persona.

In almost exactly one hour that is the face she too will adopt.

When her mother died, Clara had made sure that she had taken the 1970's coffee table from her parent's house. It is low to the ground, laid in brown tiles interspersed with occasional swirling red tiles like galaxies. Her mother kept this table tidy; she kept everything tidy, took great care, except of herself - she had let herself rot away. Clara's feet rest on it now amongst the unopened letters, football trading cards, smears of dried modelling clay, junk mail, pizza leaflets - life is too busy to tidy the detritus. Her heel nestled against the Sunday supplement left there weeks ago when her mother-in-law came to stay. Only old people buy Sunday newspapers - or newspapers. On the front is a picture she recognises. She nudges it out.

Changing Rooms: Repairing and Restoring. How Anglesea Abbey was brought back to life.

Late July - only two months ago.
The grass, dry, higher than her shoulders.
Sweeping arms through it.
Childlike.
The rub and cut of stalks against the skin, the bristling against fingers.
Sun full on her face - opening her, filling the hole.
Ahead the house, tiny, in the swathes of parkland.
The vast empty lawn.
Strange to call it an abbey.
This is the time and place to be alive - she thought.

Wandering dreamlike along the long lanes of mown grass, adorned with naked gods here and there.

She found the wicker dome deep in the parkland forest - dream dome they call it - in which she sat. Around the woven wicker cage, plants had grown so birds landed above her head unknowingly watched. Something about the structure kept the sounds of the external world away and the small voices of the birds amplified within this little place.

She was herself. Entire love and joy of herself.

That was just two months ago. Since then she had not felt love or joy or a sense of herself. Only drudge, and fear and the hole that sits right there in her waiting for her to remember it - most evenings, all weekend, every morning. But you can't just make joy come back. Her therapist says, you won't always feel this way. Yes she agrees but doesn't believe it.

Lipstick face on.

Morning lovely. Up you get. No you dress yourself. There's a smudge on that. Come on - leave that. Well have a wee then. Leave the Lego. Later when we get back. Shoes. Teeth. Come on. A snack? What for? You get snacks in after-school club. Well that's cos you're fussy. After work because it's not Friday. Supermarket. I'll pick you up. Daddy's sleeping - leave it. Tomorrow. Daddy does tomorrow. Me today. Come on. Cold today - coat. Keys yes. Oh thank you sweetie - it's nice to get a compliment. When someone says a kind thing to you. Did you? Good. Good. Yes. Come on then.

Today she arrived at work with no recollection at all of how she got there. In these days of the absent mind, teleportation is a thing. Cars drive themselves, people arrive. The journeys are made in the mind - of data, and meetings and imaginings of lessons, and conflict, and how that person still won't have done that thing. And the board, and the Trust, and the money that was there but now isn't. And the door that needs fixing and the fire escape that is broken. And the Maths teacher that needs appointing. Parking space: DEPUTY HEAD.

Each day begins as a variation of this.

One thing that never happens is this: she never goes in room EB12. Never. She cannot bear the walls, the seats, the smell, the carpet.

That is her Manderley, her Chesil Beach, her Bourton, her East Egg.

She deputises everything that may take her to that room. Everything.

It was her decision to repaint every classroom blue and cream. It was her choice to take down all the framed-bloody-pictures of sports cups for this and sports cups for that. It was her choice to cover the walls with giant quotes from literary texts in every corridor because *English is the most important subject - double weighted*. It was her choice to overhaul the uniform and change the ties. These were her unquestionable, reasonable choices. Adopting a phoenix as the emblem because the kids would like the Potter-ness of it she said. But really it was the only thing she gave herself - to allow herself to remember.

Yeats wrote: "I mourn for that most lonely thing; and yet God's will be done:
I knew a phoenix in my youth, so let them have their day."

At 3.25 Clara sits in the staff toilet as usual. It is Thursday. Milk, cereal, curry (no he won't eat it), chicken, salad…just see what is on the shelves. Staring at the back of the door. At the back of the blue plastic coated doors she chose. Not focused - on nothing in particular. And the hole in her middle of her begins to stir. She pushes it away.

Lipstick face still on. Across the car park.

Bye. Yes see you tomorrow. Nice evening. Lizzy who's picking you up - you've called mum - ask at the office.

Between work and pick-up and supermarket, somewhere, a smell of something unfathomable, but a sweetness, enters the air. Clara is whirled back to sitting in the other seat in the front on her way to Edinburgh, in her best friend's car. That was almost exactly probably six months after her baby came. This journey was the only other time in her recent memory that she knew she had felt happy. Like the wicker cage at Anglesea, she had been enveloped and held in a space out of time. She had been in love - this time not with herself and yet also with herself. She remembered the absolute boundlessness of the feeling - like it really could happen. But she never called it love, not even in her own head.

It was impossible to think about that nonsense anymore - so she just didn't.

Okay out you come. No don't bring Rabbit - okay but don't lose him. Hold my hand. No you are too big for the trolley. Right fruit - what shall we get? That's a celeriac - umm - I don't know how to cook that. It does look like that doesn't it – "wonky football!" Grapes - you like those now do you? (Hi Steve - yes have a good evening) Someone from work. Black carrots - are you going to eat those - bit overpriced - maybe just some normal carrots. Okay. The black ones.

And on...and on...through each aisle. Choosing the things everyone will eat. Choosing none of the things she wants to eat. On...and...on

And then it happened, in this place. She has imagined it happening in another place - but not in this place. The ordinary and the extraordinary:

a baby about two perhaps left alone in a trolley contentedly messily eating a packet of baby crisps covered in orange dust on face and hands seemed to have been left looking towards an adult a father? a brother? a man the child knew. the one Clara knew. and he reached at the furthest end of the aisle for something up high and he turned and he looked at her (at Clara) right at her and they stood in suspended time for moments that felt long but were short and her stomach rose up and her breath became difficult and her skin became hot and they still stood looking till another, older man was there shaking his hand and holding a phone up and wanting a selfie the child said daddy and the younger man smiled and shook the hand again and walked toward her still holding her gaze (Clara's) deeply intensely like it had always been and she could do nothing and think of nothing and no words came to her and so they stood looking looking at each other until she broke the gaze. said come on. to her child.

and walked away.

She had thought about this young man she could see at the end of the long aisle as she glanced once, fleetingly behind her.
She thought about him on her way to Edinburgh that time, and she had thought about him in that place between wake and sleep many times. And she had thought about him every time there was nothing else to think about.
She'd seen him once two years ago, on a chance encounter, and they had gone to his hotel and held each other, talked, kissed over and over

again like they knew it would only happen then, in that moment.
They did all they had fantasised about. Talked about.
And they talked that night - but somehow couldn't say anything that answered the questions about why this hadn't happened before and why it seemed to mean so much and why their lives had moved together and apart so many times.

She had not heard from him since then. Not once.

That evening, returning from the supermarket, at home, for the first time in a long time she kept her phone next to her all night. Whilst cooking. Whilst bathing her son. Whilst tidying the Lego bricks away. Whilst reading with him. Whilst writing her governors' report. Whilst watching something with her husband there whilst he worked on something. Whilst she undressed. She-tried-hard-not-to-search-official-twitter-page. But she did. And the fan selfie was there

@-ed and #celeb #geez #myman #bestever #COYB. And a reply comment - *nice to meet you mate.*

She slept - with her phone next to her. For the first time in a long time. Listening.

Jay 2009

Jay strolled across the playground, head down. He had discarded his rucksack and blazer by the tennis court fence. He had untucked his shirt. He had loosened his tie knot and undone the top button. His football nestled in the crook of his arm, left hand on waistband.

It was September. The sun cast his late summer shadow behind him. He was only the second kid on the playground that morning.

Walking across the asphalt, thinking the first thing Oli would say to him was about his Fifa rating last night. It was. They'd been up until one playing Fifa 09. Jay thought about the fact that next season he would have his own avatar - he'd be signed for the local club at 16. His coach had promised him - basically the paperwork had already been signed.

Oli went in goal and Jay fired shot after shot past him. They swapped. Jay let Oli get in a few, otherwise the lads would stop playing with him he had noticed. Fat Josh came over next - his jumper way too tight on him - Jay passed to him, back and forth, back and forth. Oli shouted to them to try and get one past him, now back in goal.

You are shit Ol.

You are fat Joshy.

Jay said nothing; he practiced keep-ups - one, two, three, knee, foot, six, shoulder, knee, foot, foot, eleven, twelve…..

The playground filled with kids - little ones kept away from them. A couple of the pluckier Year 8s might venture onto their patch, usually Jay's brother and his mates. Today they did.

Mum's proper angry Jay. You didn't put out the bins. She'll be pissed all day now.

Soz mate. I'll text her.

The bell sounded from inside the school building. Jay firstly scooped up his ball. Then he did up his tie, tucked in his shirt, put on his blazer. Collected his bag. Then he stood by the mirrored windows in the prefab and swept down his hair, flat to the right with a flick. Until he was twelve he had had long, light brown, almost blonde hair - dad's choice - emulating his own football role models. Now the style was short - Beckham like - Dad half approved.

THE JAY IS THE MOST COLOURFUL of the crow family in the UK. With a pinkish-brown back, white throat, black and white features on the rump, wings and tail, as well as a beautiful graded stripe of dark and light blue on the wings.

>*Play at break Jay yeah mate?*
>
>*Aright Joshy - get me a bacon roll before ya come out yeah.*
>
>*What we got lesson two?*
>
>*We ain't got the timetables yet bud. Might see ya.*

As he bouldered along the corridors, kids stepped out of his way. He was a king. Everyone knew Jay. Everyone. He had said *alright mate* three times on the way to his tutor room, *do your tie up ya little skank* once - he filled the space. The walls moved for him. Once at the door of the tutor room, he casually bowed to his form tutor and handed her his football. Common routine, adopted since last spring, when Miss Green had had enough of him rolling it, rolling it under his foot against the leg of her desk. She had sat him right at the front - of course.

Timetables handed out. A plea for patience, for quiet.

You got Mr Southfield? You in my art? Miss where's EB12? Why ain't we got you Miss? I've got a blank, what's that? Didn't choose DT - Graphics. What time? Miss what does PE slash C mean? Core? What? Sharm! Miss she's ripped mine....

The teaching staff, in classrooms throughout the building, dismissed tutor groups and opened the register for the first class of the day. Most who saw Jay's name on their list would feel the dropping of the stomach, the shortening of breath, the sudden need to sigh. Warren Barnes was *bloody glad* to have him on the list - best player they had ever had at the school, ever. Barnes only struggled to stop the others in the class feeling demoralised when Jay was around - but it wasn't that Jay ever made his classmates feel that way on purpose. Barnes' word for him was awesome - he was awesome - filled him with awe. *We are bloody lucky to have him, really bloody lucky.* The PE faculty always had his back.

One teacher saw his name on the list, but it was one of many names. He meant nothing to her.

Just a name on a list.

Today at exactly 11.27 she would meet him.

She would sense him before her - before one word had been spoken between them. She would know him before she knew anything about him.

And the giant laminated Shakespearian quote on her classroom wall read:

"Some consequence yet hanging in the stars
Shall bitterly begin his fearful date"

During the first two lessons of the day, Jay was caged. Stuck in the corner of a Maths room on the first floor, then trapped in the corner of an almost windowless Geography room on the second floor. When he felt caged like this, he tended to stare out of the window, re-imagining his passes from the weekend game or working back though that goal last night in the Champion's League match, trying to remember what his dad had said was so *fucking legendary* about it. But it's hard when there are no windows. He would tap, tap, tap, tap his foot on the chair leg. *Stop it Jay.* Then he'd flick, flick, flick, flick his fingers against the text book. *Stop it Jay*. His body felt too much for the room. He would stare really hard, trying to focus. *Jay stop staring - focus.* He knew that his body was moving on its own, so he'd look at his mates to see if they had noticed. Catch his eye, laugh, wanting to impress him. He laughed back. *Right that's enough - get out- wait in the corridor. I've had it.* And he would wait in the corridor. *I cannot believe you have started another year like this Jay. I knew it. I wish you hadn't chosen Geography. If I had my choice you wouldn't even be on my list. Look it's serious now. You have to focus. Can you? Come in and get on with it.* And he would come back in. And he would try. But it's hard when someone had just told you they wish you weren't on their list.

And for some reason, he can't stop his mind thinking about his dad and his *fucking legendary.*

At break, Charlotte waits for him in the corridor outside the Geography room.
Thought we were going out.
We are.
You never texted me back last night.
I was playing Fifa.
Is that more important?
Dunno. Leave me alone Charl. Talk later yeah.
She was the kind of girl he was supposed to go out with. Thin. Long straight blonde hair. Make up. Insecure. Popular. Hot friends. All his mates fancied her - or said they did.

She sort of bored him. He didn't really know why. They sat in her room or his room or went to Nando's and usually in silence. People saw them together. It was boring. They had had sex. It was boring. But he loved her - that's what love was he supposed - boring. At the end of Year 9 he'd asked Charl's friend to give him a blow job under the Maths stairs. She had. He had wanted to tell all his mates, like they had done when the girls had done it to them, but he hadn't. He hadn't enjoyed it - afterwards he felt what he supposed was shame or something like that.

Eurasian Jay is often heard rather than seen. It remains hidden into the dense foliage, but sometimes we can see it easily in city parks. This bird is usually solitary or in small family groups. Several unmated birds often gather in spring to attract a mate.

Uncaged: flowing, running, striking the ball, the sound it made -there is no other sound the same, laughter, approval, excitement, an arm around Fat Josh, hair ruffled, the surge in the legs, the ground under him, ground, air, sun, breath, sweat trailing from his face - pooling in that hollow above the clavicle, the shouts, cheers, a voice, he has a voice, here he could focus - in this time and space. This is the time and place to be alive.

A complex wing pattern very conspicuous in flight.

And hot and wet and emboldened by his break-time flight, he moved unaided it seemed, without legs or feet, to the classroom. Here he expected nothing, knew nothing of this room. Never been here; never seen EB12. The whispers were - she's tough, she's good, she's a bitch. In the corridor, they heard her heels unseen eating up the empty air, unknowingly he made way, they lined the wall waiting for her. She moved along them, not even glancing their way, unlocked the door. Made them wait.

They shrank beneath her eyes as each student before her entered her room, her space, her time.

And he felt her in that room. Every breath of the air had her in it.

She held them there - made them silent - told them exactly how it was. Said she knew nothing about them.

He could be anyone he wanted then. She didn't know him. And it was entirely her space - her studio - her theatre - her page - her pitch. He had no desire to look out of the window.

And when he tried it on - just to test - she said *don't try it on*, like she knew.

She said: *You are Jay. Like a Jay. Jays are beautiful. Loyal. Clever. And Jay is a wonderful name - like Jay Gatsby.*

And he had no idea who Gatsby was, or what a Jay was, but he wanted to know. And even when Oli tried to talk over her, he said with his body and his voice: *shut up Ol, let her talk, what's wrong with you?* And everyone was silent. She looked at him one second, one fraction of a second, less than that, longer than she should have, he thought. And he smiled.

He had one of those rare smiles with a quality of eternal reassurance in it, that you may come across four or five times in life. It faced--or seemed to face--the whole eternal world for an instant, and then concentrated on you with an irresistible prejudice in your favor.

You even have Gatsby's smile, she said.

He got home. Mum was pissed - in every meaning of the word. He played Fifa. He texted Charl. When Fat Josh texted (*football at the rec?*), he replied he couldn't.

He'd left his ball, discarded, in EB12.

Messenger - one chat head conversation

Friday at 01:21

JB: Hey

Friday at 06:01

CH: Hey. Think I saw you yesterday.

Friday at 07:05

JB: You too.

JB: Couldn't stop?

Friday at 07:07

CH: I had to get back. Life's busy. What you doing back here?

Friday at 07.15

JB: Few days with the fam. You ok?

Friday at 07:17

CH: I'm good! What you been up to?

Friday at 07:20

JB: Football, football, football. As usual. Your kids cute.

Friday at 07:22

CH: Yours too! You got a baby?

Friday at 07:25

JB: Mia. She's 15 months.

JB: I remember when my bro told me you were pregnant.

Friday at 07:32

CH: Seven years ago now. I thought you'd hate it.

Friday at 07:34

JB: No I knew you would be one day! Didn't change anything.

JB: What you doing today?

Friday at 08:20

CH: I'm at work. The day job!

Friday at 08.22

JB: Shame. Till when?

Friday at 08.28

CH: I have meetings after work.

CH: 5.30

Friday at 08.30

JB: Heading back north then. Home game Sunday.

JB: Still think about me?

Friday at 09.02

CH: You know I do.

CH: Still think about me?

Friday at 09.05

JB: You know I do.

JB: Ever think about what happened?

Friday at 09.24

CH: Of course. You?

Friday at 09.27

JB: Most days.

Friday at 09.30

CH: When you back?

CH: ??

[You cannot reply to this message.]

Clara 2019

Clara scrolled through the messages again from Friday. From Jay.

Good. I'm glad I can't talk to you. It's pointless. It hurts. Best left where it was.

But the hole is here today, like yesterday and Saturday. Bigger than ever. Or as big as it was after the last time.

Clara sits in a meeting. The room smells of new buildings and catering sandwiches. At one end is a blank white screen, one you roll down and clip to the base. It fills the entirety of one end of the room - the long board table pushed right up to it on that end, distorting its screen. And the projector not humming, but whirring in over-heat. The windows open eight centimetres. Two are open. Clara sits projector end. She doesn't know, but her breathing is almost non-existent. There are twelve Heads of Faculty in the room. At times like these she feels like laughing - like when she stands in front of a classroom full of students and they are silent. It is funny. She explained this at her husband's work party once; they didn't understand what was even a bit amusing about it. Non teachers are always interested in what it's 'really like' and always raise eyebrows and say, wow it must be really tough. *You haven't got a fucking clue.*

The screen loads. It shows pictures of five line drawn buckets filled with various amounts and colours of sand/water/tears...whatever. This model represents the 'new assessment structure'. She talks. They listen. Someone sniggers at the back. Sutton, who always stares at the ceiling, stares at the ceiling: arms crossed over his shirt, the bottom of which is untucking - skin visible. One of the new ones, who's name Clara is yet to remember, is taking notes and nodding. *Don't bother love. This will all change next year, and the next and the next.* They look tired and jaded and bored. Someone makes to leave - thinks twice - sits down. Sinclair gets his planner out as if to say, I need to do the thing that is really what this job is about, plan some goddamn lessons. PE Barnes yawns loudly and stretches his whole self out, arms resting on the backs of the chairs either side of him, his groin lifting the table for a moment. Barnes was on her side once.

Clara stands up.

She says quite plainly: *Look I have not got a fucking clue what I am talking about. Buckets. Who gives a shit?*

She walks over to the sandwiches. Lifts the whole tray over her head like a waiter - fingers splayed under the platter. She throws it into the middle of the board table.

She says: *Eat. That's what you came for. The free food.*

Then she says: *I hate this place. It is taking my soul.*

Then she walks out, leaving them there. Some may have been applauding.

That didn't happen. Instead this did. Her phone lying on the table flashed up the football score from last night's match. The one he was playing in. She hadn't asked it to. At the same time the boardroom door opened - the Head was there.

She thinks: *Shit. I never did anything wrong. If he is saying I did, it is a lie.*

The Head summoned her outside. He told her to let the faculty heads go. *Email the information from the meeting round this evening Clara. One of our students has been involved in an incident. A stabbing. I'm afraid he has lost his life. It'll be on the news tonight. Let me speak briefly to the faculty heads before they leave. Then you will need to write me a statement for the press. You knew the family I think. Billy Haynes? Meet me in my office in five minutes, okay.*

He touched her arm below her shoulder. God she wanted to cry.

Billy had been one of those kids Clara always liked. He was totally out of control in any context in which he needed to be in control; that meant practically any lesson in which you were expected to sit still, listen, write and be quiet. And that was most lessons. He was almost constantly in the exclusion room which was a holding pen for those like Billy. Clara manned the holding pen at least twice a week. In there, students were expected to sit still, write and be quiet. But Clara's approach was simple - close the door and talk to the kids for one hour, tell them to turn around and be quiet just before her stint was up. They always did. This was not school policy. But in there she never had a to throw out a student, fix-term-exclude anyone or call for back up - except once when a girl said *you are a cunt and I am going to kill you*.

Billy looked very young for thirteen. This is what happens in areas of huge social deprivation - the kids are small. He had white blonde hair and very blue eyes. His skin promised the freckles he'd have if he ever saw the sun.

He always went to the shop on the way to school with a fiver from mum and bought five packs of biscuits - the really cheap bourbons and custard creams.

He always gave a whole pack to Clara on exclusion room days.

The kids in the holding pen had one thing in common - they would talk about trivialities for around twenty minutes: what YouTube videos they'd seen, what tattoo their siblings had got, how Mrs Arch was a bitch (sorry Miss, you probably like her). No comment. Then they would begin to unravel. It would be the scary stuff: the drinking at home, which often also meant drugs, and the abuse, neglect, the knife gangs they knew, the brother in prison coming out. And it would trickle out shaded in laughter. But Clara knew what it meant. If they never got that time with her, when else would they talk?

Sometimes an official writing-up of a worry, abuse, concerns, a safeguarding referral had to be made - but often nothing tangible was said.

Billy would come and find Clara sometimes when he was chucked out of lessons. It wasn't just him: Krysal, Connor, Fial, Danielle. Because she would listen. She couldn't fix it. But she would make them safe for a few minutes.

The job is hard when every day feels this way. Before it wasn't like this. In the past, the kids came from another part of town. Then they built the large new school and expanded another. The whole town seemed to shift. Ten years ago, as a classroom teacher, the worst

Clara had to worry about was a few mouthy boys and too much marking.

Jay was one of the mouthy boys.

Billy was a different breed.

And now he was dead. It seemed impossible.

In the Head's office she always felt uneasy. She sort of liked him and was in the strange position as a senior leader that meant he was the only person she could confide in, about anything, but she never did. The only real confidant she had was Fraser – even though she wasn't supposed to have any 'friends' amongst the staff body. The Head often referred to the staff as 'the employees'; Clara was expected to view them in the same way. But she had known Fraser since her second year as a teacher. He was totally reliable. The Head was made of corners and boxes. Fraser was complicated - that comforted her. The Head was affable, predictable, but totally devoid of human emotion.

The boy was killed in a knife attack, he said.

Billy, she reminded him.

Yes. Billy apparently stabbed with his own knife. How many times have we run these sessions telling them not to carry knifes? I mean we have done our bit haven't we?

Well Billy was probably in the exclusion room that day or truanting. They are the ones we need to reach sadly aren't they.

It's unfortunate he was fix term excluded yesterday. It's possible the press will pick up on that.

Don't worry. I'll deal with it.

You know - the party line - just reiterate the policy.

If I have to. I think perhaps something heartfelt and compassionate might be the first comment we make.

Yes of course. I'll ask the parents in for tea on Thursday.

Maybe we can hold a memorial here? Perhaps we need to think about a permanent tribute to him. A bench or a tree?

I don't think the budget will stretch to it Clara. Maybe a fundraising later in the year. He was into that football club wasn't he - the big one - one of our exes play for them I think. A lad you taught I think.

Maybe we could get him here for the funeral. That would be a nice touch.

Possibly. I don't know who'd have his details. We permanently excluded him if you remember. I doubt he would do us any kind of favour.

Did we? Well I'll ask PE Barnesy. I think he'll have his details. He's twenty five, twenty six Clara - he's probably over it by now. Anyway it didn't seem to hold him back. Ha!

Clara's therapist had noticed something fundamentally mind screwing once: *You don't actually know what your feelings are do you Clara?*

This was one of those moments.

So floating above herself she could observe something - hotness of the neck, short breaths, deep deep heaviness of the stomach, a tingling pain the lower arms. The walls sliding to a tilt. This may have been sadness for Billy, for his family, for her family, for knowing Jay would refuse to come, fear at the mention of him, the rejection, the sadness, the utter sadness. Something else - her mum, her husband, herself. Death in there.

Our death.
All of our lives and our deaths.
Because we live. And we die.
And what futility the in-between is.

That evening at home - after dinner, bath child, read stories - Clara emailed the PowerPoint about buckets to her staff. How utterly trivial that seemed now. And she drafted a press release:

Billy was a highly valued member of our school community. We are all saddened by this tragic event and our thoughts go out to the family at this very difficult time. This terrible loss reminds us all of our need to remain committed to educating our students about knives and understanding those compelled to carry them. A tribute will be made to Billy by our students and staff later in the year. May we take this opportunity to remind the government and our Trust, and the governing body that exclusions are often the result of poor funding. How can we operate a system that supports our most vulnerable students when we are stretched beyond our capacity as a staff body? It is impossible - so kids like Billy end up out in a community in which they are drawn to crime, or at least feel they have to protect themselves from those who before them were thrown out of an education system allegedly designed to help them become functioning members of society. We cannot do our jobs in this broken, self-serving, target driven, short-sighted system. We have no choice but to exclude students like Billy because we have built an educational structure in which these young people cannot survive. We failed him. You failed him. Society failed him. Rest in peace Billy - I'll miss you. And your biscuits.

She deleted it from: *May we take this opportunity*…..and emailed it to the Head for his approval.

Jay 2009

Jay was straight up the English block stairs, passing Miss Green his tutor on the way, barely seeing her.

God you are early! You ok? Ball's in my room. Miss gave it to me yesterday.

What is this feeling? A sinking.

He found his ball in his tutor room, behind her desk, as Miss Green had said. He took it outside, kicked it hard, really hard, against the wall where he was not supposed to - not because he was not supposed to but because it was a hard, towering surface. Told his mates he didn't want to have a kick-about this morning. He was glad when it bounced back, smacked him in the shins, in the thighs, on the stomach once.

He didn't speak through registration, not through Science either when he was usually pretty lively, bantering with Mr Moles. PE after that and even then he still felt some of that feeling that made him want to hit something. He pushed and pushed his energy, his swirling-ness, heaviness, into the basketball game. He shoved Freddie right into the wall. Kicked the ball into the corner grunting when he missed a basket. Josh asked him what the fuck was up, at some point. *Fuck off mate.* Nothing else to be said.

At break the English teacher was on duty right by their patch - the other side of the tennis courts. She looked cold. She held her cup between both hands like it was an offering. He approached her, looking away. Jay held the ball tight to his chest, arms folded across it. He held it to stop, to stop himself throwing it at her, to stop himself saying: *look at me, watch me, fucking notice me.* His head was down as he passed her and then he looked up, over her, past her -nonchalant, looking for the pitch where the lads were. Close to her, passing, she'd sense him like he could feel the aura of her as he slowed just by where she stood.

Get your ball back Jay? Gave it to your tutor last night. Didn't want you to lose it.

Pause. A kindness….

Thanks miss.

The concrete that had been setting around his arms, fists, ribs lightened; cracked. He was okay. He dribbled the ball to the field just beyond the courts - toe, up, heel, knee. Turned to see if she'd seen. She hadn't. Didn't matter.

After Maths he had an incredible desire to find Charl and kiss her or fuck her. But the first would do. He waited outside MA06 for her - top set always out late. She rolled her eyes at him through the glass panel as Mr Salar set the homework. When the door opened, Jay pushed Charl against the glass and kissed her hard. People laughed. He turned to smile smug at them - still pinning her.
Aw-rite laaaad! It was Oli - from the same class. Smacked Jay on the back.
They caused a bottle neck there. Mr Salar moved them on, whilst Year 7s went by trying to make themselves small: squeezed in behind the crowd into the classroom.

Jay and Oli shouted - *There's only one Mr Salar!* - repeatedly until the sound faded down that corridor.

By the time he got to English at the end of the day he felt out of control. He knew the class were being difficult - making it hard for her.

She stood waiting, waiting for them to be quiet. And stood. Arms crossed - she looked at the clock - again and again she looked at the clock.

Why didn't she shout? He wanted her to.

They would laugh if she did - she didn't though. She just waited. It was a bit weird - like she didn't give a shit.

Then she came and stood right next to him, hand on his chair. It was a threat. He could feel the warmth of her. He couldn't look at her. And she blocked his view of Oli.

The whole class sunk down.

They got serious - tired.

A hot air balloon landing. A table cloth being laid. Floated softly down.

Some kid read from the book - he strained to take it in - *Street after street, and all the folks asleep — street after street, all lighted up as if for a procession and all as empty as a church — till at last I got into that state of mind when a man listens and listens and begins to long for the sight of a policeman.*

She asked them what was the significance of the door in this chapter of Jekyll and Hyde. Oli was being a twat - asking what significance meant. She calmly replied - meaning, importance.

Jay put his hand up. Looking - seeing he was the only one.

Well it's like a double meaning right - blistered old door like no one cares about it - also shows what the person inside is like. Dirty. Nasty.

She said that was good. Felt good that.

They had to write about that door then, it's significance. He wrote - wasn't hard. He watched her sit with some girl, lean over Oli at one point telling him he was doing well, pointed to the book when Kristen asked for a quote. He wanted to stop looking at her. So he gazed out of the window - looked at the field - watched a figure walk a dog along the pavement.

Her arm was next to his then. She sat right next to him. On the chair right next to him. *Come on Jay. You alright? This is good what you have written. What you thinking about?*

He lied - said he just wanted to be outside -playing football. She didn't move. Thought a flicker of hurt crossed her face.

Write another one - like that for me - look at that quote maybe. What could you say about it?

But it was too late - he was gone now. She didn't stay - moved on - complimented someone else. Now he watched the clock.

Books in the box at the front. They wait in silence. He wants to go - doesn't want to. Bell sounds.

As he passes her, she puts her hand on his arm - *well done today, good work.* Hands him the ball she'd taken at the start.

Suddenly and without any sense of it building, he needed to run. Down the corridor dragging Oli and Freddie along. Hearing Mrs Green telling them to calm down from her classroom door along the corridor. Out. Out the school. Out the gates.

Home - laptop. Search - Horton - Clara Horton. Profile pic. Holiday photo on a pier. In silhouette. Just the silhouette of her form, legs. This account is private. Request? No fuck it. Twitter. Same name - not her. He'd seen her laughing with Mr Moles once in the corridor. Search Moles - Jamie Moles - James Moles - JJ Moles. Photos. Picture of her and him in pub? She's kissing his cheek. He's squinting? Winking? At the camera. She looks fun. Funny. He's a cunt. Log out. Google search - Hort... - nah - search Champions League.

Jay's brother Liam comes in. Chucks his school bag onto the sofa knocking Jay's arm. Slumps onto the other chair.

Training tonight? Mum says I gotta come with.
Why?
Dad's workin.
Bring your PSP.
Got homework - can't be bothered though.
Who you got for English?

Fraser - he's decent. You got him?
Nah - Horton.
Supposed to be a bitch.
Nah she's alright mate. Got our arses kicked. Nah she's good.
We gotta go in 10. It is training innit?
Yeah. I'm gettin my kit.

Mum at training - not watching - on her phone. Liam pen in his mouth - nudging mum - she ain't no help Liam lad, he thinks. He has not played well. Coach talking about the match this weekend - not gonna start ya mate if you can't focus. *Empty as a church. Empty as a church.* Be alright by Sunday guv - he says. Sort your head out kid.

Dad gets the full rundown by text. Livid when they get in.

All we ever wanted for you, me and ya mum, was for you to make it big. You fuckin know that. Brought you here to this shit hole cos the club was good. You got a chance here - don't wanna waste it. I had your talent - gramps didn't give a shit. All about fuckin rugby bollocks. You know that. Why ain't you on it

Jay? Sort it out. Your brother ain't got a scrap a talent in his body - look at him - reading a book. That ain't gonna get you a Rolex mate. Ha! Fuck's sake Jay - you are a fuckin let down. Get to bed - don't wanna look at ya.

In bed. He'd liked she'd taken his ball to keep it safe. He liked her saying what he said was good. He liked she could control the room. He liked her voice. He liked her hand on his arm. He felt like she liked him - like she understood something about him. Felt like there was some signs of something - not knowable. Maybe she was just good at teaching - yes just that.

Charl's mate texted - *Charls upset. You dick. She says u laffed at her.*

He thinks she's a dick. Can't be fucked with it. Ignores it. Turns his phone off.

"....bore in every feature, the marks of prolonged and sordid negligence" - these words came back to him in a mind between wake and sleep. And her finger nail on the page. Sordid. Sordid. Sordid.

Negligence. Not loved. Left. Not valued. Wrong. Not wanted. Dirty. Unpleasant. Need to be played Sunday. Got to focus. Get this right. Back to the day job. Gotta get this right.

Jay 2009

Jay was back on form. Better than ever. No problem playing him every Sunday for the last nine weeks, the gaffer had made sure.

There was one difficult match for him first weekend in half term, back in October. It had been an unusually hot day for autumn; maybe that was why. That's what dad had said anyway. He felt something like that feeling he'd had the day his ball had ended up - not where he'd expected. He thought, perhaps, it was because he missed being at school or something.

But it was the holidays, which were a good thing. Everyone knew that.

He had played poorly that day: unfocused, kind of angry. Kept looking in the stands but he didn't know why.

He searched for a face he knew wasn't there.

Over the holidays he had played football every day - sometimes even with Liam, just to have the practice. He'd played a lot of Fifa late into the night. He hadn't seen Charl. Never thought about her even.

She'd texted him: *don't you want to see me no more.*

He'd replied: *not really. Concentrating on football.*

Eventually the holidays ended. The Sunday night before the first day back, he felt a lightness in his chest. Walking to school that Monday, he was bantering with everyone he passed. Saw Fat Josh, slapped his back. *What you lookin so down about mate? I can't wait to get back at the books!*

But the weeks went by and he'd been thrown out of lessons, for the usual reasons. Not even bothered doing his Geography coursework. Finally in detention he'd typed out something about sea defences and coastal erosion. Knew he'd get an E for it - just his name in the top seemed to guarantee that.

But four times a week, when English came around, he was buzzing. He graciously handed his ball to Miss at the start of every lesson, sometimes with a wink or he looked at her, right into her eyes. He thought that did something to her - he loved that, was gaining something in this room, time after time. Each time he felt the bubbling stomach, the lightness in his arms; soon it was time to try something new.

One step more.

They had had coursework at the end of the Jekyll and Hyde unit. Oli had hung back one day after class, saying, to be honest Miss I ain't got a clue what I'm meant to do for this. She'd offered to help him after school next day. Jay knew he couldn't let Oli have this alone, so out of solidarity, like a good mate, he stayed back that afternoon too. They'd bantered with her, teased her. She was maybe uncomfortable, unsure of them. Her whole neck from just under her chin down to the top of that green fitted dress she wore had gone blotchy pink. Probably further down. Oli had said, *come on mate let's listen to her; I gotta get a B on this*. So they had settled down and she, to be fair, had made a lot of sense then.

Jay had stood, wide legged, hand through his hair. *Ol this is easy bro.* He already knew this stuff - even the quotes he'd use. *How does Stevenson express to his reader the duality of man? You just gotta get ya head around chapter ten Oli mate,* he'd said. *Fuckin easy then.*

She'd said, *thank you for your wise words Jay. You always put it so eloquently.*

I got a lot a skills miss. You ain't seen half of them yet.

She smiled, sort of trying not to, he thought. Went and sat behind her desk. *Just get your work in on time boys, then I'll be impressed.*

He had delivered his work to her room early one morning, imagining on the way to school, down the corridor, that she'd be there marking something. Her desk was in the corner. The opposite end of the room to where his chair was in the class, by the window. Maybe she'd have her pen in her mouth. She'd look distracted, thoughtful, like she did. She would gaze up at him as he strode in and slid his work along the desk to her.

He'd imagined the rest too.

But when he got there, she wasn't in. So he left it - wrote his name in pencil. Rubbed it out. Found a post-it and just drew a love heart on it. Put it on the front page. Took it off. Stuck the post-it right in the middle of her white board. And left.

She never mentioned it. But he noticed she kept the post-it on her planner. He asked her once, *who gave you that.*

I don't know actually, she said, *probably Mr Moles. He's always doing that sort of thing.*

His work got marked. She gave it a B. He wondered how biased she could be. But his form tutor even mentioned it in tutor time one morning: *we moderated, that means checked, your work last night Jay in our meeting. It was very good. Best I've seen from you. Well done. You get on with Miss Horton don't you.*

Bloody love her Miss.

It was November. He'd be sixteen this month. Life was shifting.

One day he came to class. Sat in his usual seat. At some point, she moved him to the front corner behind the door.

That same lesson he sat with his feet on the chair opposite his - he shifted it back and forth. He couldn't quite see her now from his seat - he had to look around the girl next to him; some quiet, geeky, fat girl called Charmaine.

Miss joked with him as he pulled and pushed the seat again - *exercising your calf muscles Jay?* He took a chance then: *Miss I've shaved my legs. Wanna see?* She laughed but not offended. Like it was genuinely funny. *No Jay: I don't. Why would you do that?* Everyone laughed then. *Makes me run faster.* She came over and looked then, as he rolled his trouser leg up to the knee. He sensed an unease around the class. But she was really laughing, with tears and a smile she was trying to straighten.

Weeks passed by and Jay worked hard. Poetry, which he'd never seen the point of before, became pleasant to him. Solving the puzzle of the message in each poem under the comforting waves of Miss Horton's voice was warming to him. Like those days as a little kid at primary school when story time began.

He was safe there.

In one lesson, they read a poem called Follower. Miss showed them a few pictures of her dad on the whiteboard. Told them he was a writer. Told them how proud of him she was. She was in some of these photos too. One of her wedding day with her dad looking up to the sky as he held her hand and the expression on his face seemed painful. In another he was with someone who was most likely her mother - this woman looked serious, like the worst of Miss Horton's faces. She didn't mention her mother all lesson.

She was strange to them that day. They revered her more then though. They felt for her. *My dad is old*, she had said. She struggled with her words a bit when she read: *but today it is my father who keeps stumbling behind me, and will not go away.*

In the silence that followed, Jay said, *you okay Miss?*

She bit her lip, staring at her empty hands. It was a moment only.

And he felt an aching in his throat. He turned his chair from under the desk and faced her.

She came and stood nearer to him, hand on the back of Charmaine's chair. Something was almost there. His muscles felt powered - he wanted to reach her.

Then moving away once more to her desk, she said, *I'm fine; just human*. She picked up her board pen and carried on.

He left his ball with her that lesson. Heard her shouting after him - *your ball Jay*. He ignored her. *You left your ball mate*, said Oli.

He didn't turn back.

But later, after school, he went to get it.

He knew the rule; he didn't close the door as he went in. He knew other kids, other staff were around. He didn't want her in trouble. But he stood against the door frame - watched her at her desk, looking at her phone - elbows resting against the wood. How thoughtful she looked; he saw the line of her zip running between her naked neck and hips.

She sensed him, saw him.

You come to get your ball? Twit. I shouted after you.

Sorry. Yeah. Can I have it?

The ball was under the desk to her left, by her foot.

He came over, stood by the right side of the desk. His hand resting on it.

She stood up. Pushed in the chair. Bent down to get the ball.

He was right there behind her. He took in her whole form, all of the back of her. He watched her hips expand as she bent.

Then she straightened, turned. Faced him. Ball held out, just, in front of her.

He stepped forward. He placed his hands on her hands. The ball between them. And so it was. And so it stayed. He tried to read her face.

Skin tingled. A shifting feeling in the chest. He swallowed.

She looked away, down at the ball.

He took it from her. But stood, a slow smile came to his mouth.

Thanks, he said. His voice low.

She said nothing.

He walked home. A story came to him, a fable from his childhood, about a bird dropping stones into a jar of water. His gaffer had mentioned this to him once - just keep dropping in the stones Jay and one day you'll get what you want.

When he got home that night, there was a letter waiting for him. It was on the club's headed paper. It addressed him as Mr Burton. At first he thought it was for dad. He let his bag fall to the floor, dropped it off his back. He stood by the table for a while, his hand on the letter, unsure whether to open it.

Dear Mr Burton.

The letter stated that the club would like to sign him as a professional player, as of his sixteenth birthday. Educational commitments could be addressed in a meeting relating to his contractual obligations which would be held on 13th November 2009.

Dad, dad, he shouted. *You seen this?*

No one seemed to be home.

"But today it is my father who keeps stumbling behind me, and will not go away." Heaney's words swept into his mind for a moment.

He felt like this was the time and place to be alive. He wanted this. He wanted to impress. Dad would be pleased.

Anything he wanted could be his.

Anything.

Keep dropping the stones Jay.

Clara 2019

A child had died.

A child.

The mood at school had shifted.

Support rooms were set up.

Students, mostly from Year 8, but other kids too, went from lesson to escape into the space which allowed them to grieve. Some went to talk to counsellors, trained volunteers, the school Police Community Support Officer, anyone the school had found qualified to listen. Some went to be silent.

Clara had gone to the support room herself - but this was a space for the children. Mostly during the few moments she spent in that room, she heard them say, 'why'.

Those who barely knew Billy hurt. It was loss - a losing - a vacancy. Tragedy; it speaks so raw. Our own mortality laid before us.

But there was another sense, a sense of electricity. A rubbernecking, gawping, voyeuristic aliveness. We are alive. He is not.

For Clara it was this: Billy had been there and now he wasn't. He was a body, mutilated, in a morgue. He was a space where there had been a something. When she brought him to mind, he was there again. The shape of him had gone, but the whole of him hadn't.

You know when I really felt it Clara? said her colleague, *when I saw it: in the classroom, the empty chair.*

The funeral procession passed right by the school. At eleven, senior staff, teachers who knew him and a few friends lined the pavement outside the school gates. Faces of children could be seen looking down from classroom windows.

As the hearse approached, it slowed down. Stopped.

The parents and cousins, little sister and uncle, stepped from the following cars and stood in the street. They were people. Clara saw the genuine human reality of them - borrowed suits, tattoos, the Mini Mouse t-shirt and pink skirt.

The tiny little girl hanging from her dad's leg as his shoulders shook, face to the ground.

What brings a family to this?

The middle of a housing estate. In the middle of a busy city. The whole street became silent.

The approaching bus stopped, turned off its engine. The noise of traffic was far away as if heard though double glazing.

Everything dimmed.

Just the birds - that was all.

Clara cried - not swallowing her absolute grief. The complete tragedy.

She looked at the coffin. It was decorated with Marvel characters and the badge of his favourite football team. It was tiny. Who paid for the coffin, Clara thought. She remembered choosing her mother's - the cost.

All flesh is grass.

Very slowly, the procession moved on, the family walking behind.

Clara entered the crematorium with the Head. It was full. Every space was taken, people stood, even in the porch way. Seats had been reserved for the two of them at the front, the other side of the aisle from the family. Clara saw her seat - Deputy Head . It was next to one with a note on it that read Jay Benson - he had not yet arrived.

All at once she was numb. Nothing - no feeling. Her body had decided. Exhausted - there was only a cloudiness. *Self-preservation though detachment*, she heard her therapist say.

The family came in along the aisle - patted, hugged on the way. The little girl squeezed up to her dad - rested her head on him as they sat. Moved her head to her mother when the dad bent down, face in hands, elbows on his legs.

A murmur began as Jay slid in from the back, thanking and apologising as he stepped past those standing at the side. She looked briefly and away again. Behind her she heard a whisper of his name. Then came the feeling: a tingling between her legs, a rising flutter through her stomach. She breathed deeply - momentary relief.

Everything she had ever felt before.

And he sat down beside her.

Then they stood again - the coffin was carried in. An uncle, a cousin, some other relatives as well, carried the tiny box. They placed it a little too heavily on its stand. No one trains you for this, Clara thought. The minster came over - placed a framed photo of Billy on the top - he was beaming in this picture, fishing-rod in hand. Dad made a grunt - animal-like.

Then, unable to restrain, no more holding, people sobbed, wailed even.

A child had died.

The minister spoke of the tragic loss, cut down in his prime, a child, the innocence of youth, loved school, fishing with dad, looked up to his brothers, part of the community.

You know nothing.

Fanatical about his favourite team. The minister looked to Jay. Everyone did. Clara didn't - she felt him move, perhaps to return their stares.

Billy was deeply loved by his family and by the community.

Was he? Then how did this happen?

"Now we invite Clara Horton, Deputy Head of Billy's school to say a few words."

Standing at the lectern, the coffin to her left, the flushed faces of the family directly in front of her, she felt exposed. Her dress suddenly too tight, her neck too naked, her hair too short, her voice too small; a fraud here amongst the people who knew him. But she knew him. And what she had written was bullshit; it was teacher-speak-training-funeral-googled-bullshit. She folded it up and dropped it to the floor.

Fuck it, she thought.

And she said, *Billy was a bloody pain in the bum.* (They laughed).

That's a fact.

He was always getting into trouble at school and I'd be lying if I pretended otherwise. You know that.

But I adored him. He was real - a real kid with a real voice.

He told me, school ain't for me miss. I can't concentrate half the time. I wanna be playing football and making stuff, not writing about Elizabeth the First and some Spanish shit. (They laughed again).

I spent many hours with Billy, usually in the exclusion room, but not always. When he was thrown out of lessons we would walk and walk and walk around the school.

He loved it.

Sometimes he'd stand behind me like a miniature guard when I had to tell kids off, or he'd ask if he could tidy my classroom or even once, do some book ticking for ya miss.

He was wonderful, funny, crazy, lively.

But we don't run schools for kids like him.

These days kids have to fit in boxes - Billy didn't fit in a box. I never imagined I'd see him in one. It is terribly, terribly sad.

Billy I will miss you.

You made me laugh. You brought me biscuits. You were kind - you were scared - I feel like you wanted me to help you. I'm sorry if I didn't do enough.

Watch over us Billy and remind us, when we need to be reminded, that boxes are not good and that we should break them down.

I will hold Billy close to my heart for the rest of my life - I feel like he has showed me something about myself.

And I hope that his tragic, tragic death will show us all that we cannot continue to let knives take our young. Let that message ring out, beyond these walls, beyond this city and be heard by those who can make change.

*Dearest Billy - may heaven be full of bourbon biscuits and football and fishing. (*They applauded. She touched his coffin.)

Then the tears came. She was crying for all the losses. As she returned to her seat, she had to look at Jay; his seat was next to hers after-all. Through the cataract of tears, he was distorted. His eyes were like they had been so many times - looking unwaveringly into hers. After she had sat, and the tears dripped from her cheek to her chest, he took her hand and held it in his. Squeezed it. She looked at his hand on hers. And the tears came harder.

All the losses.

And yet some of these tears were about relief. A warmth spreading from her stomach outwards. Upwards. Her chest filled with it.

Then it was over. His hand moved away, but slowly, regretful. Before anyone saw it.

She thought back to a time many years ago when he had put his hands on hers. Around the football. It had been awfully wonderful. Bewilderingly clear. Painfully comforting. And she had fought herself to never think of it again after that.

He never gave up on her.

But more challenges came and she pushed them aside, inside, deep within her and she got through that year.

He never gave up on her.

It ended so painfully.

He never gave up on her.

But more challenges came and more. And more.

Learned behaviour - she had got used to pushing him away. *I don't deserve you. How could someone like you have any feelings for someone like me?*

Her therapist had said, after the time, the last time, *Don't you think he might love you? Why wouldn't he?*

Why would he? she had replied.

Couldn't you be his love? His fantasy?

No. He pushed me away.

Do you push him away? Have you ever ignored him? Have you even denied him something he wanted?

Then came that feeling. The one where she wants to change the subject, manipulate away from this. Her brain dances off to other subjects. This is important - drag it back.

I had to deny him what he wanted because what he wanted wasn't appropriate.

When?

When he was sixteen.

And what about when he was twenty-one, or twenty-two, or twenty-three? Wasn't he an adult? Why deny him then?

Because I was married. And I had a job to think about. A mortgage. A child.

Interesting. You haven't said, because I didn't want to. What did you want to do?

Change this subject. Look at the flowers on the windowsill. Are they fake? They must be. They never change.

Clara closed her eyes.

I wanted to see him.

And you said no.

Sometimes we have to.

Do we?

Yes…I was scared. Clara was crying.

Can you imagine that perhaps he felt pushed away? Perhaps he felt hurt Clara. Perhaps it broke his heart. First love. Perhaps you need to sit with this - it is hard to see what he sees in you isn't it? Ask yourself why that might be. Ask yourself what you are scared of.

After the funeral, people drifted away. Clara spoke to parents and students, some from long ago, who said *good speech* and *you've always said it like it is.*

Had she?

Sometimes it is hard to see yourself because the mask you wear has become part of your skin.

Coming to the wake? they asked. She hadn't intended to. Before she left this morning, Clara had known that she wouldn't attend the wake - that was for the family. But she had changed her mind - she would go - leave behind the box she had made for herself.

Standing between the bleak, whitewashed walls of the community centre.

Tea in a white cup with a white saucer. Cheap cups make the contents cold.

Laminate floor - pine. Chairs - blue padded metal.

People grouped into old, cousins (young), cousins (older), bystanders, onlookers, strangers, the nest, family, parents, siblings. Teachers.

Clara watched Jay. He was statuesque in this place where most were grey and bulging. He was alive where others were tired and cold.

Every man and boy in the place wanted to touch him - on the arm, shoulder, back. Shake his hand.

Clara looked at his thighs, hands, lips - *I've touched them. They me.*

He was the warmth in this room.

This doesn't seem like the place for some mega star sensational footballer does it really? said the Head, moving to stand next to her by the bar. *Do you remember him from when he was at school?*

A bit. He was very good at English.

I heard he was a shit. Excluded for, what was it, inexcusable rudeness to a senior member of staff?

Yes. God these days we'd exclude pretty much every kid if that were still a legitimate reason. He didn't really do anything wrong. They just never liked him.

So he was a shit.

No he wasn't. He was just hard work.

Oh. En guard! He's coming over.

Hi Jay. How's life? Meet Charles - Head Teacher. I'm good. Nice to see you. Under the circumstances. Yes still at the school. Ha ha! No I'm Deputy Head now. Thank you - that's kind. No, I never thought I'd be Deputy Head. Some. Still teach some English. Are you serious? You tell people that? One of the biggest influences in your life? Ha! Wow that's very kind. Did you hear that Charles? Ha! You should give me a pay rise! I'll look it up. I didn't realise you'd mentioned me in any interviews, let alone that one. Wow. My son? Yes he's fine. How about you? How's your family? Yeah? And how is Liam doing? To Sheffield? Very good for engineering they say. So not far from you in Manchester - you see him? Liam went to the school too Charles - Jay's brother. He was very good at science. How's the club and all that? Great. Yeah well obviously I see you on tv now and again. We are all very proud of you.

Must be strange though to think you are a commodity. Something to be bought and sold until you are not good enough anymore, Charles said. From nowhere. The place he comes from when his social awareness button has been switched to hibernate. *Have you thought about what you will do when it's all over? Clara says you were good at English. Perhaps you could be a writer.*

Actually, I have a degree in accountancy. So I'll do something with that....Shall we get out of here? Let me take you for dinner...Miss.

Jay 2010

It was May. All of life was football. Jay knew the exams were coming. But he didn't care.

Three days school - four days football. That was his life now.

What he ate was about football. What he thought was about football. His body was football. His talk was football.

Since January his whole life had changed. Now he had two days training in the week - at the academy, the real thing. Drills and practice. Gym. Sports psychologist. Dietitian. Media training. Sauna.

Each afternoon for two hours, he was with a tutor supplied by the club. He only ever did his English work. Some weeks Miss had sent nothing over. When her work was there on the desk with a note on it - her handwriting - he imagined the words it might say. Or a phone number. Some weeks the tasks to complete never arrived, he had to remind her - *I need work miss so I can keep up. Don't wanna let you down.*

It was all part of the game.

Only a few more pebbles.

The water was rising.

The time was coming. There would be a flood.

He was in school only three days - that was two hours of Maths, three Science, two GCSE PE and two English. And six other lessons he barely even bothered with. Dad's words: *you're gonna be a fucking famous footballer mate. Ha - you don't need to know about how many women some old king was banging!*

Jay didn't take History anyway.

Just before Easter, Miss Horton had been away on a residential with school. What he knew was the same feeling as when the season ended - an emptiness. Something made him say to Mr Moles in Science that week, *bet you wish you were on the residential sir.* Moles had thrown him out when he laughed and said, *you'd be having fun with Horton. Bet you want to don't you Sir!*

That day he had been isolated with the Head of Year.

*Way out of line Jay. Way out of line. Don't push your luck. You are not liked Jay. You are lucky to have made it this far. An exclusion could ruin your career. We made an agreement with your club. Don't get arrogant - ha - more arrogant. Don't push me Jay......*on and on and on.

When Miss came back, he had gone to find her. She was on duty in her usual place by their patch. Usually he ignored her, but thought he saw her watching. Wanted her to. Today he felt something shoving him, so he just did it, went over and said, *don't do that to me again. I missed you.* She smiled with one side of her mouth - she'd said, *I'll try not to.*

The flood was coming.

A clouded distance was there between them in class. Maybe it was because the end was near. Soon he wouldn't be candidate number 1642. She wouldn't be loco parentis.
He knew it.
She must know it.

After that it would all be different. And so they went through exam paper and exam paper; he worked hard.

At parents' evening she had told his mum: *this boy is a pleasure to teach, he could get an A.* Miss was charming. Smiling. She had spoken to him, as if no one else was there, brother and mother evaporated: *when I first met you, I knew you'd be trouble. You have surprised me. I am very proud of you.*

Mum had been strange that night.

When he really thought he knew, arrived in a moment - only a second perhaps. The class had one final piece of coursework to complete. It was a study of the opening few scenes of a film called Atonement. Tension - that was what it was on. How the director had created this tension. The buzz of the bee, the tick of the heels, the music, the lighting, the clipped dialogue.

In tutoring, Jay had sat with the man who wore the waistcoat and the club tie, who probably did it for free tickets, who he thought at any moment might ask why he only ever wanted to study English in these sessions meant for every subject, but who never did and seemed glad of the fact. Jay had written a long essay - longer than allowed - had to cut it down. The waistcoat man helped cut it. He'd told Jay it was very good. Worth a B at least.

Comments on the essay in Miss H's handwriting: *Wow! Jay! This is astounding. You have given a personal interpretation in which you have used appropriate reference to techniques and you have made judicial choices of examples to illustrate intelligent points.* He got an A.

But that was not when he thought he knew.

After the essays were done, they had watched the rest of the film. She has made sure it was in the two lessons he attended that week. Often films bored him. This one bored him. But at some point, something happened.

The bit with the letter - the mistaken letter - that letter felt like his letter. The way the letter said *cunt* but it was beautiful and sensual, not an insult. Just a part of the female body.

Sweet. Wet.

That man, Robbie, felt like him.

Unseen, not knowing how to move or speak, feeling so fucking much.

When the two characters who have felt so much but said so little are there in the library, against the shelves, Jay caught her eye. She was looking at him. In the half darkness of the room, the light of the screen, she was.

His sixteen year old self could not know that that was an image he would live, and relive and live again and again. Two bodies against a wall. Him holding her.

In that moment, he thought he knew.

What is it the girl said in the film? *You knew it before I did.*

Now it was May. Last game this weekend. Last lesson this week. Once next week came, the Year 11s only came in for exams. He'd missed the whole year photo - on one of his academy days. He wasn't going to the prom. The lads were going but the Head of Year had said he couldn't attend. Another punishment he didn't give a shit about.

Fat Josh had said, *you should just turn up anyway. Like ask your club manager to bring you in his Porsche. That'd be well funny.*

I don't wanna go Joshy. Ain't got a date. Ain't gonna ask anyone. Anyway who gives a fuck?

You should ask Horton. Ha ha! Seriously mate - you really fuckin fancy her!

Yeah right. Can you imagine? Fuckin Moles'd be cryin all over his specky face!

Imagine her gettin out of that Porsche with you - knowing you're gonna fuck her later! She'd love it.

I'd fucking love it!

I reckon you could tho.

Nah! Leave it Joshy mate. She's not gonna do that - she's a teacher. Fuckin love it tho. Anyway, I ain't allowed to come to your gay prom mate so that's that.

And that was that.

Except Jay thought about that fantasy over and over, building it up, making it real. When he made himself cum, it was her. Between the porn. Not always. Nearly always.

Friday came. Jay felt unusual.

This was his last day at school. Forever. Except exams.

Tomorrow the season ended.

There was a buzz. And a odd unknowing.

Everyone was crazy that day - out of control. The girls were crying. People were in a kind of hysteria. Others were distant. Jay felt sort of sad that he wouldn't see people, even those he never spoke to.

Something bigger than himself was coming to an end.

Him and his mates had been trying to think of something funny to do to mark the end. Like everyone does. The stupid new Deputy Head guy had told them in assembly, any acts of defiance will lead to immediate exclusion. Even on the final day. They hadn't managed to think of anything funny - thought about stripping the Head Boy and tying him to the school gates. But that'd probably get them arrested.

Horton had come up with an idea. Actual genius. Just before break, like ten minutes before,

Jay and Oli and Josh and Anneka and Krystal and Connor, had just got up out of their seats in their classes and started a conga. That was it. All around the school. Kids from every year came out and joined them until they were in one long disjointed line. No one could pin down who started it. So no one could get in trouble. Even some of the teachers, in some kind of rebellion, joined in. It was mad and wonderful. After not long it all fell apart. The early flourish of joy gone.

Then they had a shirt signing. Jay didn't go. He didn't want to remember this place. Of course he would love to have Miss sign his shirt, feel her hands on his back or his stomach as she wrote some poignant goodbye.

But she was already tattooed on his skin. He felt her under it.

After the mad flurry of the morning, they had to settle to lessons. Miss had said, *sorry guys but it is your last lesson before the exam, which is the first exam. So no party lessons for you this year - sorry.*

The final lesson came.

But a stupid thing had happened.

Maybe if they laughed it off, everything would be ok.

Oli and Jay came into English laughing about it.

Did you see her face tho? It was really funny. Oh come on Jen, it was funny! Look we were only messing about. Yeah well she didn't have to be such a bitch about it. Seriously it was a joke. Miss, right, basically a load of us picked up Miss White, you know the teaching assistant, and carried her to the middle of the field at lunch. It was funny! Like no one started it. It was funny. Head of Year is after Jay for it though. She still had her sandwich in her hand! Oh so funny. Like when she was shouting, put me down. Oh brilliant. Legend.

Horton smiled, but was not amused. She cast her eyes down. Looked serious. She said she hoped the school would forget it. That they should get on now, just focus.

She was pissed off.

That was not intended.

Not an outcome they had expected. Not even thought about it - in the moment, buoyed up with the madness.

The lesson began and it all seemed to fade away. But Jay was quiet. He wanted to be quiet. He felt that strangeness come again.

The door opened. Very suddenly. Head of Year. *Come on Jay - bring your stuff. Sorry Miss. I need to take him.*

But why? What's he done? This is his last lesson.

Yes. Sorry. Get your stuff now. Come on.

He did not want to go.

Stop this happening - he thought - looking at Miss Horton.

She thinned her lips. Shook her head. Her eyes saddened. *You'll have to go Jay.*

Fuck. Someone pulled his fucking heart out.

He was walked to the new Deputy Head's office, down dark corridors.

Body so tense. Fingers digging into his palms. Lip held tight.

He stood, absolutely not understanding what he was hearing. Looking at this stupid fucking man. Fucking cunt.

Right. That is it. You cannot treat staff in this way. I know you started this ridiculous prank. So you have done it now. Your parents have been notified. You have been excluded. Permanently. You will be escorted on and off the premises for exams. You are not welcome on this site. You have had too many chances. That was the last one. Your mother is coming to collect you now. Make your way downstairs.

Jay said, *Yeah? You are a cunt. Fuck you.*

Then his body took command. He pushed, with both hands, the woman behind him. She stumbled. This was his Head of Year - aghast. *That was a big mistake. We will have the police escort you. Come back.*

He ran.

Into the quad. Surrounded on all sides by two floors of windows, grey rough concrete.

He went the way he thought they wouldn't follow, into the building across the square to his right.

Up the Maths stairs.

Back up into block EB. Mr Barnes was there, waiting for him. He had his hands on both hips.

Benson, come on lad. You have to just leave. From his tutor room, just down the corridor and to the left, Miss Green came out. *What's going on Jay? Are you in trouble.* He knew they were on his side - but he was being caged in.

They were moving in on him, tentatively.

His arms worked without him. He punched the wall. For a moment he was surprised when the plaster cracked. *Fuck this.*

Jay walked straight past them. Opened the door to EB12. Went straight in.

They've excluded me. That's it. I'm out of here.

There was an audible gasp. Oli shrank, worried he'd be done for too. The kids said stuff, but he heard none of it. Jay walked straight up to Clara. She'd already begun to move toward him. They stood together before the class.

I won't see you again. This is it.

They held each other. Bodies hard against one another. Both of their arms, their hands, pulling one another in. It was seconds. But it seemed minutes. Later, it would seem like a second, no more.

Jay. Take care of yourself.

I'm gonna miss you.

When they looked at each other, Jay looked past her. Not meeting her gaze.

He was crying.

The Head of Year came in then: *Right. Come on. You have to leave now. The police have been called.*

All of him wanted to stay in that room.

But he left.
And that was that.

Clara 2010

Clara sat down on the bed in the hotel room. The room smelled of dead cigarettes. And the tinges of brown in the corners stated that this had once been a 'smoking room'. Of course now there was no smoking anywhere on these premises.

Shame.

Clara was feeling empty.

The promise of this trip had elated her to begin with - her first residential, her first chance to prove she could plan it and risk assess it, get the coaches booked and the rooms sorted and the right kids chosen to make this easy. And the chance to be away for a few days. No planning and teaching and struggling and marking and cooking and exercising and tidying and pushing those kids for grades.

But now she sat alone on the bed, wondering how many times the purple, satin coverlet was washed. She felt busy, restless in her own company.

The students, all from Year 9, were nice kids. They were the 'gifted and talented' - most were geeky, middle class. A couple were the 'disadvantaged group' who had to come to fill the government requirement allowing the trip to run and to be subsidised. They were, as it turned out, the most in awe of this trip. One of these girls, Danielle, had said to her as they passed along the Embankment, *Wow! I've never seen a river. Is this the one from Eastenders? My nan said it was*. Astounding, endearing, to think some of those kids had never seen London before. They were a short train ride away in their own city, but they had never been given the chance to visit.

Most had stayed in a hotel before, on holiday somewhere. But none of them had stayed overnight in London. One or two had never been away from their parents.

The innocent are humbling.

Clara hated most of the staff at school, other than Fraser and Jamie Moles who was fun to flirt with and fancied her. The others she thought boring, ill-educated, culture-less, pedants. When the kids had asked her which teachers she liked and didn't like (kids always took pleasure in knowing those secrets), she would say, *I don't really like teachers. They are boring.* Of course she was supposed to say, something about professionalism, and colleagues and respecting all staff. But she rarely followed the rules.

Most kids liked her, respected her, because she was human.

So for the trip she had selected: Barnes (reliable pair of hands, good bloke), Shawcross (young teacher, nice girl, light timetable, not much cover needed) and Fraser (her friend - easy company).

Clara had just taken out her travel DVD player and was thinking about watching an episode of Sopranos. Something to take the emptiness away. Fraser knocked on the door: *Come for a drink. Julie's on student watch. Barnes is calling his daughter in Dubai or something. Anyway, let's go down for a couple.*

There was a pub right across from the hotel. A 'micro-brewery' which Fraser said was this new fashionable thing to do. Brew your own beer. Clara thought it sounded like her dad's attempts when she was a kid to make homebrew, or elderberry wine. But the place was nice, homely but stark, quiet.

Clara was dressed for a school trip. Jeans. Fraser was dressed as usual in his shirt, tie and work trousers.

Fraser, I am surprised you don't wear that when you go out back home. Probably pull more girls if you did. What happened on Saturday after I left you guys?

Me and Stella went to the club. We were wasted. Seriously. She is hilarious though. No idea when I got home. She was upset about how she didn't meet any blokes - again. I remember that.

She gives off the wrong vibes. She needs to worry about it less. Did you pull then Fraser?

Nah. Not this time. Kids are nice on this trip aren't they. Cute how excited they were by the TVs in their rooms! Asking, can we watch them? I said, what else are you going to do with them? Ha.

You gonna miss your Year 8s? Little shits.

No! You gonna miss your Year 11s?

No. Not at all. They'll miss me though! What's Benson going to do without me? He's so funny.

Still flirting with you is he? Did you ever report that exam paper? The one which he covered in love notes?

She laughed, uncomfortably.

No - no he was only joking. Hoping it would get him a couple of extra marks he said. He's alright. Harmless fun. I have to keep him on side - no one takes it seriously. Honestly he makes me laugh. Better than when he was a miserable shit all the time. He's fine with me. Never plays up. Everyone else seems to hate him though.

Yeah. The new deputy was saying the other day they are looking to get him out. Make an example of him. Probably an excuse to stamp his authority. Like a Prime Minister starting a war. It's all politics.

Really? They had better not. He doesn't deserve it.

Clara went quiet. They had better not.

You alright?

Yeah. It's just unfair. Anyway that new deputy head bloke Cranford, I don't like him. He said to me he thought female tennis players should play with pink balls. What does that even mean? And he forgot my name the other day, which is fine, but I mean who does he think he is? He watches surfing videos all day in his office, I heard.

While the rest of us are working our arses off. They are all the same Clara. Want one - cigarette - outside?

They spent another hour bemoaning the senior leadership team and sharing life advice. Fraser asked her once again, as he always did, if girls thought he was boring or too nice. And she said, he was a nice guy for the right girl. She always said that.

The following day, they toured the British Museum. That was what they had come for - a special educational trip to see the new exhibition about Aztecs and another about Italian Renaissance painters. The students went off on their tours and workshops. The teachers traipsed along behind.

Oh bloody hell, said Barnes at some point mid-morning. *Just got a text from Steph. Jay has been isolated for the day, pending possible fixed term exclusion. Stupid boy.*

What's he done? Clara's throat contracted. She swallowed.

Been rude to staff, again. Riling your mate Moles. Jay's an idiot. I wish he'd learn. He struggles to control himself. I tell them this all the time.

Clara said, *he is so good in my class. I don't get it. People just don't get him. He's a good lad - he's bright actually.*

Yeah well he likes you so you're ok. He's not like that with everyone. You and I know his arrogance is a front. We both know what his family are like. He's just gotta keep his head down and get out of here so he can just do football.

I don't want him excluded. He's on for a C at least.

Barnes held her upper arm as he looked at her, with a genuine compassion: *Well talk to him. Maybe you can make a difference. You should.*

Clara promised she would. She told herself she would.

She never did.

Maybe that made all the difference.

Clara arrived back late on Tuesday evening. That morning they had visited Kensington Palace. Queen Anne and her lovers, her many dead children. Princess Margaret and the man she couldn't love - duty and appearance. Clara thought of all those broken hearts - trapped women. After the coach arrived back at school, she waited until the last parent remembered to collect their child.

When she got home, her husband was in bed asleep.

There was an emptiness - a vast cavity growing filled with a wrenching. She'd known this feeling before. As a child.

She slept it away.

On Wednesday, a very unexpected encounter threw her. But it also took the emptiness away - filled it with a buzz. Jay had strolled over to her on duty - she was thinking about her next class, what she had planned. He was standing right by her, smiling his one sided, almost shy, smug little smile. Then his whole face straightened - his eyes intense - as she had seen before. His height, his form made her feel younger than him. *Don't leave me like that again. I missed you.*

A heat flooded into her neck.

She felt herself half smile: *I'll try not to.*

The bell rang. She smoothed her feelings out - closed that one down. Breathed the tightness out her chest. Put her cold hand to her hot neck.

For the past three years, Clara had known the mixed feelings that come in May of the school year. The oldest kids in school leave and this is sad. Some of them, most of them, you will never see again. Not many people can know how the emotional investment you have put into these students leaves you with a grief when they go. Any human would feel that. Most, honestly, are forgotten in a few weeks - the joy of the space in the timetable, the summer evenings, the promise of the holidays fades the shadow of grief.

Some are never forgotten. They appear as a fondness when the time comes to teach that play or poem again. Clara kept their notes and scrawlings and strange little gifts. And now, in this new time, they appear on timelines and statuses and tags.

Clara would be glad to never see some of this cohort again. And desperately sad to never see others. They had been a struggle. She had hated them collectively at times; woken up dreading their defiance, negativity, stubbornness. Once the black dot of Jay Benson was on her side, some of that faded.

Many years later, her therapist would tell her, as a hyper-aware emotional being, Clara could sense the mood of thirty individual kids at a time. This made her an excellent manipulator. But it was exhausting.

She had gone to the shirt signing. Felt the excitement. Written the usual: good luck, keep in touch, you were a pleasure to know….always the same. She had been amused when a conga line of one hundred students or more passed her door - that had been her idea - Connor , a boy she'd taught in Year 10 last year, had asked her to join them as he ran past her classroom. She declined.

She had to get these Year 11s to focus today. Final lesson before their exam. She planned to deliver an intensive revision of all the texts for the first exam. Final period, final day, she knew she was up against it.

As they fell over themselves into the room, there was a sense of anxiety.

And a silliness.

And a subdued quiet from some.

The lads explained an event that had happened at lunch - they had carried that bitchy teaching assistant who was always telling other people how to do their jobs and had once questioned Clara's professionalism over some comment she made - they carried her onto the field and left her there. It was funny. Well deserved.

But Clara was worried. Saddened. It was heady with anticipation - not right. Something not right was there in the room.

And Jay was all of it. He was quiet, distant, palpably coiled. He was unknowable that lesson.

For all of them, the walls bounced back static.

She talked. They listened. Made their notes.

The door burst open. Clara hated that - this was her classroom. Her sense of superiority, authority, undermined as some frizzy headed woman she mostly avoided, dramatically swung back the door. She demanded Jay go with her. Entirely inappropriate - inconsiderate. He had a bloody exam on this - that was more important right now than some silly incident on the field.

Her mind said: *Fuck off you shortsighted fool. Who cares about that right now? No. You can't take him. He is mine.*

He is mine. You can't take him. I don't want you to. Don't take him from me now. Don't.

Jay looked at her - his eyes told her to make it stop.

She couldn't.

Her position made her powerless. And when faced with idiocy, ego, misplaced authority, jealousy, politics - the powerlessness is made greater.

She felt certain he would be back. She knew it.

Kids have an unadulterated sense of knowing. They have not yet been self-taught and shown by society how to ignore the innate emotional communication we receive from other humans. They know fear and frustration, excitement, desire. They know when you are present, and not present. They feel it, mimic it, become it - they adhere to tribal instinct to feel as the leader feels.

And there in that classroom, as they looked to her to know how to feel, they knew her discomfort, her anger and her panic - was it panic?

But what she painted about herself like a disguise was - let's forget that happened and get on with the revision. *Come on guys. Forget that. There's twenty nine of you left who have an exam to get through.*

Miss, what's going to happen to Jay? Asked Oli. Concerned, sadness in his voice.

He'll be fine.

She ached. Felt a pulling away. Like her chest was being sucked to the floor.

Right. Let's start with the poetry. Key words - let's start with Follower - what do you think?

They had never been softer. Never more subdued. There was a suspense as they wondered, all wondered, what was happening in a room somewhere - wherever Jay was.

Minutes later he was back, but not how she had expected.
Not with the calm of an apology, a misunderstanding. Like the door had opened before, when Jay had been summoned, it did so again without restraint. It banged against the wall - did he know it had? Desperately he exclaimed to them all, something about this being the end. Being kicked out. Reliving this, in time, Clara couldn't remember the exact words. Only the static in the air grew stronger, something was dying.
It was not supposed to end this way.
She wanted to pull him back, keep him there. Her body reached for him and she knew him then pressed against her, his hands tightening on

her back, a grasping between them. Such unexpected loss. Such a yearning…for what? He slid his mouth to her ear. She thought he would kiss it; said, *I'll never see you again. This is it.*

Against her he was shuddering, vibrating - feeling it was anger, she should soothe him.

Sensing it was tears.

Nothing had ever felt like this before.

And all she felt on her tongue, she could not say. Something bland came from her - some words that meant nothing. All the feeling was in it; she wanted him to know that.

I'm gonna miss you.

His words circled her head long after that moment. That grief, that loss, that longing and fighting, that realising of everything before denied, the pushing it down, keeping it at bay, the professional front, the never let it in, that knowing and feeling and not-believing. That was the pain she felt when Jay walked from the room.

That was the pain she had, for a long time, to drive away.

Jay 2012

Jay was in his seat, on a table with his manager, the coach and five of his team mates in this auditorium – white table cloths and round tables below a stage set out for the ceremony. There was a relaxed anticipation around the room. Jay's palms were damp. He rubbed them on his trousers as the league chairman rose to the podium, shook hands with the two hosts on the stage. Cleared his throat. Began to speak, reading from a piece of paper he drew from a gold envelope.

Since signing for the club last year, Jay Benson has delivered where is counts: decisive leadership during his many caps, quality play on the pitch, valued support to his team mates and the clear determination to succeed despite the setbacks of an injury last season. We see a great future for you Jay. And so with great pleasure, we award you Player of the Year. (Quietly, on stage to him): *Well done mate. Well deserved.*

Jay had stared at his lap for the entire build up to this - the other names, the other clubs.

He'd hoped. He wanted to win this. Spent nearly a grand on his suit - looking hot. Looking the part. Nervous though. Tightness where he breathed. Still felt the place, just along the left side of his ankle where the tendon had snapped. It was the jabbing ghost of a pain.

His whole team and every other team in the league were in some grand old theatre by the sea. In a town that wasn't his home. The tacky local DJ hosts and the rolling stomached mayor, the sponsor boards and the club colour balloons above each table made the place look gaudy, brash. Corporate. But that was the game - money and brash falsity - that was football.

He loved playing. The rest was just how it was - what he'd grown up with. Like some child star acclimatised to the glittering trash of Hollywood.

The stage made him nervous. He felt his tremor - the one that he thought gave him away. But no one ever seemed to feel it, notice it.

It was Jay's turn to clear his throat. *Thank you. I have enjoyed my time at the club and the lads are family now - aren't you boys. It's been a tough season - some big asks of us this year. But we did it. I'm looking forward to our next season in the next league - bring it on hey boys? Thanks again to the club, the lads, coach and of course the supporters - wouldn't be here without you. Thanks.*

What did all of that mean? He hadn't thanked his physio or his girlfriend - or dad. He'd do it later. After this photo. This next award. This drink. This night out in town. This drink.

This one.

One more.

This next bar.

This woman he thinks he'll pull. Older than him.

This drink.

This shot.

This arsehole he can see by the bar. This conversation he can hear. About his club. lucky - lucky to be promoted. played shit. fucking overpaid gay boys. ain't got any talent between ya. come on then.

This fight in this street in this town this punch in the face this kick this fucking kick in the ribs.

These arms pulling back his arms. This fall hard on the pavement.

The police were called. He was arrested.

Bailed out.

Driven back to the club office. Slept in his suit in the manager's Merc.

After this meeting with the media manager. This hangover. This panic.

He'd thank them then.

This meeting back at the office with its off white walls and signed framed shirts.

We will struggle to keep this out of the press Jay. This was the media manager, Steve. Grey trousers, grey thin jumper, shirt with the collar plain and the body striped. Grey hair - prematurely. *What were you thinking? You won't make it like this mate. If anyone calls, don't answer. Or no comment. Pass it all to me. We'll manage it. Not sure how we will cushion this one mate. Hopefully pay the locals to keep it quiet and I'll pull some strings for an article on your award in the nationals. Keep off social media - like I've told you before. Be careful. No private accounts. No private conversations. It's all traceable. Just phone calls to family for now. Okay?*

Jay watched Steve's phone on the table. A ping. Photo of some woman - not his wife - popped up - love heart emoji. Fucking hypocrite.

Jay got his girlfriend to pick him up. She didn't speak to him all the way home. He pulled his cap from the back seat of their SUV that smelled like she'd just had the Polish car wash boys in it and on it and inside it. One of those toilet cleaner scented cardboard trees hung from the rear mirror. Put the cap over his unwashed hair. Every time she looked left or right at a junction, her blonde ponytail skimmed her seat back. Swoosh. Swoosh. Swoosh. Swoosh. It was all he could hear now he had heard it. *Oh for fuck's sake Mol, calm down.*

She still said nothing. Grasped the wheel tighter.

He got home. His phone was off. Opened his laptop. Logged in to Twitter - temporarily deactivate account. Too many mentions and notifications to even consider - just close it. Facebook - a private account - deactivate it just to be sure. Feed opens - more and more notifications pinging up to his right.

There at the top of his feed - Clara Horton - pink fitted vest top, bow in her short hair, beautiful beautiful face, smiling, holding a baby maybe weeks old. Never looked so good. Never.

He enlarged the picture - looked long at it. The details of the room. A hotel? Grand blue walls, huge marble fireplace. She looked so relaxed. Happy. Beautiful.

Her eyes.

Who was she with? Whose baby? Her husband's he thought, but didn't know.

And a gripping rose in the top of his stomach. A pulling. Then his jaw tightened. He felt his back teeth hurt.

Deactivate account.

Closed the laptop with force.

Got up. Paced the flat. Kicked the sheepskin rug by the fake fireplace. Stood by the window in his bedroom overlooking a car park. Growled and grasped the air with fists holding nothing.

Fuck this. He shouted it. His girlfriend left the flat – he heard her slam the front door. The guys he shared with were out - still enjoying the sea air back where he'd been dragged from in the early hours.

He fell face first onto the bed and growled again, whole body, into the pillow.

Then he cried. Not sobbing tears. Just some welling in his eyes - burning from his chest.

Fell into sleep.

Steve had called some favours in obviously, or someone had. Jay got a caution. And it appeared in the local paper read by two hundred people in this seaside town. 'Blues Brawler Gets Caution'. Few online comments. Didn't make it national. A week later, Steve constructed a genius campaign across the media – 'Blues Boy on Top'. The sexually suggestive headline got hundreds of thousands of online hits with a shot of Jay mid run, bottom centre left, eye drawn to it. The story told of future accolades, future signings, future success.

Good story on ya lad. In the papers.

Thanks dad. Yes dodged a bullet there.

Keep your head down lad. Seriously. That anger has gotta go. I know how it is. You know that. I'm not proud of what I did in the past. Red mist innit lad. I'd have hit anyone - not proud of what I did to mum and Liam. But I learned. Or else you lose everything.

I know. It was stupid. I won't make any more mistakes.

When you and Molly gonna visit then hey? Mum misses ya.

I'll try dad.

Family. Always family first. Remember that.

Something about dad's repeated phrase - family, family, family - stuck in Jay. It was a phrase he used himself - even tweeted it. Some residue of guilt sat in the lines of those words. And a helplessness.

A vision of his mum, drunk and bruised on the kitchen floor appeared like in a video game. He shut it down. Thought of her alone most evenings. Dad betting. Dad always used to be in the betting shop, or now at his mates houses online watching sport, any sport, and jubilantly dancing home to her telling of his winnings; or sneaking home shamed. Angry. Either way, she'd get left to sleep if she was lucky.

Jay probably should plan a visit.

In bed, he fantasised about going home. Bumping into Clara, Miss. In his fantasy, it was as she came out of school. Picking her up. Her hips bigger after the baby. Tits bigger. Eyes wider. He held her hair, pushed her mouth down hard on his cock in the back of his car. Fuck, he loved that thought. Then she'd look at him from between his thighs and say *You are amazing Jay.*

He wanted to contact her. Couldn't. Too risky. Not allowed. Plenty of reasons not to.

But maybe it *was* time to start dropping the pebbles again.

Monday was his day off. Gym - the songs on the gym radio all seemed to be from school days. He thought about Clara. Threw his bag on his back seat - saw Clara there. Put a bet on at

Kempton on his betting account - lost. Remembered the feeling of loss. Opened his phone once he was home - logged onto Facebook - deleted all notifications without reading any.

Two choices here:

Delete her - block her - pretend you never knew her.

Message her. Just to see. Just in case. Drop a pebble into the jar.

Messenger

Monday at 5.50

JB: Hey. Miss your favourite student?

He waited. Checked. Put it down. Picked it up. Checked. Left the room. Went for a piss. Came back. Checked.

Monday at 6.20

CH: Hey! Good to hear from you superstar!

CH: Of course I miss you. Miss your favourite teacher?

Monday at 6.27

JB: Of course. More than you can imagine.

JB: Still think about me?

Monday at 6.30

CH: Yes Jay. A lot. You?

Monday at 6.35

JB: Yes. I miss you.

Monday at 6.36

CH: Me too.

Monday at 6.40

JB: What you been up to?

Monday at 6.42

CH: Not much. Just had a baby.

Monday at 6.44

JB: Really? Nice one.

JB: I think I saw a photo.

Monday at 6.45

CH: I saw a story about you someone shared with me. So proud of you.

Monday at 6.47

JB: Thanks. That is good to hear.

Monday at 6.57

JB: You know I always fancied you at school.

Monday at 7.05

CB: Yes I know. Well you had good taste.

Monday at 7.11

JB: I did. Still do.

Monday at 7.13

CB: Have good taste or fancy me? Lol.

Monday at 7.15

JB: Both

Monday at 7.19

CB: I'm flattered. You are a beautiful young man.

Monday at 7.21

JB: So are you. Beautiful that is.

JB: Wanna meet up. Just get a coffee or something?

Monday at 7.30

CB: I can' t Jay.

Monday at 7.32

JB: Why? Can't you say you are seeing a friend or going for a jog or something?

Monday at 7.39

CB: Maybe

Monday at 7.40

JB: At the weekend? I'm back home.

Monday at 7.51

CB: I can't. Sorry seeing friends.

Monday at 8.15

JB: Lol. OK.

Monday at 8.16

CB: Sorry. I really want to.

Fuck it. Block her. Fuck you. Shouldn't have even bothered.
Jay felt stabbed. Squeezed. Hurt.
Forget it.
But he felt it. All night. All the next day. It was taking his mind away from life - from what was real. What was this feeling? What was this dull ache? Why didn't she want him?

Maybe it was money. He needed more to impress her. Maybe it was his hair. Maybe it was the size of his cock. Maybe her husband was better than him. Better. Richer. Better looking.

But some part of him knew. Couldn't mistake the pull, the urge, the pain, the grid of something bigger than him. It told him, she does want you. She means it - *I really want to.*

Too complicated. More than he could understand.

Next week him and Mol were going to Dubai. He'd buy a Rolex. That'd show her and the rest of them what he had. Then he'd try again with her.
Drop a fucking diamond studded stone in the jar.

Clara 2012

Weeks of: milk feeds from a bottle and nappies changed to wake him and to sleep him and endless walks pushing the buggy down paths and alleyways never before walked down by her or sometimes anyone it seemed. Lunches and baby groups and really fucking dull conversations. And box sets. And the loss of who she had been. Further and further into a place where she became as dull and dulled and dimmed and extinguished as all those other insipid watery mothers. But the routine killed the monotony. And the wine helped. The challenges she set herself of getting her baby to sleep at this exact time and drink this exact amount of milk…helped. Something goal oriented to focus on.

She had read Jay's words, *Miss your favourite student,* and she had felt lighter; relief - a relief of heaviness long held.

Coffee was not a coffee. This was the edge of something - the end and the beginning. And she couldn't meet him. That she could, and she might, and couldn't and shouldn't, held the conflict - in resistance. In there too, a fear he wouldn't show up. Let her down.

And because new mothers were not supposed to meet beautiful, young, successful footballers. Because she was fatter and her stomach was no longer flat, her hips were bigger, and she was ugly.

Not good enough to meet him.

The shouldn't was mightier than the could.

She googled it - you cannot reply to this conversation. He had blocked her. Or so it said on the answers her laptop was giving her.

So the heaviness returned. And a hole appeared in her stomach - so it felt - one you could slide a hand right through.

Before this moment, she had thought about him, often. She was proud and filled with something like love or warmth when she saw his successes in the media. She fantasised about him, about what could have been. She saw that picture of him with the article Fraser had sent. Jay in mid stride, a man in statuary, like she herself had commissioned his form to be sculpted for her. His face paused in joy. He'd scored a goal in an important match.

She was held against him again in her fantasies. But she did not reach out to him and had not thought about making contact because, the facts were, he had forgotten her.

Then she had read, *Miss your favourite student*. It was a thread, a string, a tissue of the thinnest most delicate petal or leaf that held them together in a moment that was charged with the same buzz as before when he had looked at her. Then in that classroom. Where feelings were confused, and they didn't know what was what.

Now there was promise and lust and honesty. And he held out his hand to her. But she was not good enough.

And after this moment, worse than before - she couldn't contact him even if she wanted to. Severed. Sawn off. Cut down.

And so like the times, so many times, she had been rejected by her mother or father or husband or the other almost lovers, she locked it out and locked it down and made herself forget it had ever happened.

A mistake. Don't feel it. Carry on.

He thought about you, well that's nice. Now he isn't. He regretted it.

You aren't enough.

It is your fault.

Shame.

How's babyhood going then? Her best friend, Nina, had asked her one night on the phone. Clara sat on the hard stairs of her house between the blaring TV noise of some shit gameshow and the intermittent crying of her baby who wanted to be fed or cuddled or changed or none of those things but an unfathomable want for something even he didn't understand.

Actually it's really fucking boring, she had said.

And at that Nina and Clara had decided to have a weekend away in Edinburgh because she needed it. And why not. Her husband could do the feeds and the nappies and the walks and the monotony for a weekend. Four days in total. Two with his mother on hand to help out.

The night before she left, dozing again on the sofa, out of boredom and the wanting to numb herself with sleep - 9.43 pm, a message. Jay: saying she was beautiful and that he wanted to see her. He actually said, like he had known, he liked her body. Didn't care it was bigger. Asked for a photo.

She wasn't ready for that.

They talked for hours through the night, through the feeds. At one point he said, I really want to fuck you. She felt the blood pulsing in her groin, over her clitoris, strong deep in her buttocks. The softening melting pulsing of her labia.

He said he had always wanted her, known she was it. The one.

The car, the desk, the places he'd wanted to touch her, taste her.

When she left in the morning, no one was there to say bye. Her husband and baby asleep. The bottles made - instruction on top of the steriliser. Food already cooked and labelled in the freezer.

Alone in the hallway, coat on, suitcase by the door, Clara felt disgusted with herself. She would know, one day, this was guilt - given to her by external forces, and by expectation, the projection of others' fear.

As the car pulled up on the pavement outside, the red brake light distorted through the mottled glass of the front door, she felt like someone standing by the sea on a September day. The promise of getting in that car was like the promise the warmth, the floating, the pleasure of the sea - the knowing of the chill of returning to shore. Because she would have to return.

Clara pulled up her collar, took her bag. Closed the door behind her and didn't look around.

But even then, despite the notes and the food and the guilt she had felt at leaving them, on the way, her husband complained that she had taken the car keys by accident and how was he supposed to get anywhere. *Walk, take the bus, the train* she said.

Spoiled it.

Edinburgh was a haze, a daze of hard blocks and black topped towers. Of a walk that took them above the city to gaze upon the blaze that glinted from the river and the windows and the glass.

It was drinks and meals and a burning to tell her friend about Jay. But she couldn't do it. The morality felt wrong - she'd never understand. Nina's life was perfect - nice little house, job, mum, dad, husband. No orgasms.

There was nothing to tell.

There were other people she'd tell - she knew partly to brag but also to make it real. It cannot exist if it has no audience. But make what real?

Clara felt a liquidity, a melting, warmth. Smooth calming of the days at home. The sort of fear she knew of getting it wrong and the invisibility, her nothingness, that was gone here, with a friend who loved her and asked again and again, *are you ok?* The flat they were renting above the Grassmarket was old and was reached by a spiral staircase. The streets surrounding them, the buildings, the market square itself and the little archway that led to their flat reminded Clara of scenes from Stevenson's writing, or Dickens: with the grandiose and the broken together.

Clara had chosen the room with a view over the rooftops – they appeared leaded and secret. And the towering Gothic steeples gazing down on her. At night, she read in bed and pulled the fur throw up around her. She enjoyed the muted laughs and shouts and sirens, amongst the silence of her room. And the silence of her head.

She and Nina strolled around the Botanic Gardens; Clara felt utterly peaceful. On the Royal Yacht she was drawn again to the stories of broken women. The photo of Princess Diana hugging her boys made her cry - god that spoke to her.

Clara was feeling. Honest, soulful feeling. Not the dulled out misery of days and days before.

Strolling around the museum dedicated to Mary Queen of Scots with its puritanical carvings of men and subservient women, Clara felt the thrill of sin. She felt the buzzing again, like rising, flushing blood in the neck and chest. She danced with ideas of Jay there with her instead of her friend - the way he'd look at her, as he always had.

All of her wanted him.

But below the thrill was loss and grief and sadness. And the hole.

Impossible.

On the way back home, she messaged him. *Meet me?* He said he definitely wanted that. *When?* She asked. No reply.

Half an hour later, she just sent: *Jay?*

Nothing. No reply.

She was quiet in the passenger seat as her friend talked about how her own baby wouldn't come and how there were tests and pills and a fear it would never happen. Clara blurted out then, *you don't have to have a baby you know, just because everyone says you should.*

Nina was silent.

You seem strange, Nina said after a while in awkward anger, *don't want to go home? What is it?*

Clara told her she had had a little flirt with someone else. It was nothing. Just made her feel like things could be different.

But they can't be different Clara. You have a child and you are married. You can't do anything. Tell me you won't. Just forget all that.

And so once again, the pleasure of freedom tumbled away. And in its place were the doors of her house. The steriliser. The sofa nights of shit TV. The shape of a back in the bed with her. And the glow of her phone in the night which told her many things but never what she wanted. And she never knew why.

Every time the same pattern - and every time she never knew why.

Now it is November. Six months since Edinburgh. Since she felt anything like happy.

Clara sits forward-facing on the train. A crowd, a swarm it feels, of young Asian couples surround her. Their language lilting but alien in her ears. The distinct smell of a full nappy makes its way down the carriage. Not her baby. One of the crowd has a baby. Someone thrusts a loud nursery rhyme video on a tablet in front of the baby's face.

Clara's own child sleeps in her lap. She can't remember when he cried. Not like that baby. That baby wants some peace, she thinks. Clara wants some peace. One of the party opens a window. Too cold air rushes in - sits on her shoulders. Her own baby stirs. She strokes his hair. Your baby needs a routine, she thinks.

She hopes someone gets off at this stop. Or this one. They are all heading to London - everyone in this carriage it seems. Clara and her boy are meeting her parents.

She feels the usual stir of pain and hope. And a hole in her middle where her soul should be. Maybe this time her mum will be kind. She might love her. She might affectionately hold her - tell her how proud she is.

Maybe she will say, it's okay. Everything is going to be okay.

Perhaps her father will calmly hold hands with her. Both hands - lovingly - look into her eyes. Ask her how her life is, how is work, and actually genuinely listen to the answer instead of reeling off his list of pre-prepared questions. Replying, *that's nice.*

Maybe mum will warmly, proudly, cuddle her child instead of being all filed nails and *oh, I can't hold him today. I'd love to but I can't.*

Perhaps dad will play with him, dangle a toy, read a story, instead of talking, talking about cousins and second cousins and friends of friends she barely knows.

Today could be different.

Clara takes out her phone. She composes a message. Why not?

Connection - someone - to be affirmed as real.

That thing that says she cannot reply has gone and a flashing cursor in the message box is there. *What you up to today?*

She closes her eyes. Scanning down her body. Eyes ache. The hole in her middle. The jaw feels set. Her fingers tingle.

The familiar ping surprises her - but floods her with adrenaline.

Why? Wanna meet?

Stupid. You can't meet. Why start this again.

I can't. On my way to London. Thinking about you tho.

What you thinking?

Mostly about how good it would feel to run my tongue down your stomach…

And so it went - down the stomach, over the maps of the hairs of his body, kissing his thighs. Everywhere she wants to go; everywhere he wants her to go.

Ping - he replies.

He talks of her eyes looking up at his between his legs.

'Where this train terminates….'

Clara opens the buggy, not easily. Her boy stirs awake gently as she bends his arms under the straps. Awake, he looks around wide-eyed. Where are we?

It is tiring. The manoeuvring of a buggy through London. All the way to Kensington. To a hotel. Always Kensington. Mum, she'd have chosen it because once it was the place to be. In the days of Raymond Blanc of Dynasty of Princess Diana's shoulder pads.

The drab, tasteless, TV trash of what they thought was classy made her sorry for them. Not that she knew. But she knew that the dark bar with the shamrock wallpaper and the elevator music soundtrack was not classy.

Her parents took trips away. Dad said it was for writing. Mum said it was good to have a break from the dark North East. Sometimes it was because they wanted to meet Clara, but rarely did they come to her home. So she came to them to meet in some hotel or other, stay over, leave the next morning. Less often since she'd been busy at work.

When dad had asked her to meet them, some weeks ago, to set the date, she had tried to find excuses. But on maternity leave, there were few places to hide.

Mum and Dad were already there when she dragged to buggy into the hotel restaurant, waiting at a table in the dark dining room. Mum had a fizzy water, Dad a red wine. Her mother smiled, half looking at her, gazed beyond her as if someone more interesting might arrive in Clara's place. Dad stood up - hugged her long and hard, and sort of apologetically as he always did.

She sat for dinner. Her son squirmed – in her arms, in his highchair, at the table.

She squirmed.

Clara had missed messages - felt the vibration though her jeans pocket. Vibrating the skin.

Her mother ate nothing. Pushed around a prawn salad. Dad looked pained.

Motherhood doesn't suit you does it? More lines I see. Makes me feel better. And your bottom doesn't get any smaller.

Thanks Mum.

What? It's just an observation. At least he is well behaved. You were such a horrible child.

The hope – gone.

A child gives you an excuse to escape. Bathtime. Bedtime. Can't leave the hotel room until morning. Tired. Might not sleep well.

The bedroom was cramped. A broken, thin, plywood wardrobe dominated the room, from which a smell of mushroom seeped. Her bed felt a cold dampness, sticky, clothes not dry perhaps. She felt dirty there. As her son slept beside her, she finally looked at her phone.

Jay had created a sexual landscape. Asked, *are you there? Wanna see you. When we meeting?* Finally she replied, *next week?*

Read back though the whole conversation - all forty seven exchanges. Wet. Made herself come. Jay was there with her in that bed which floated beneath her naked back. Turning on her side; opening her eyes. Reaching out her hand.

Just the wall. Only the wall.

In the morning, Clara reached for her phone. Nothing there. No reply. She deleted last night's thread of words - gone. She could pretend then, to herself, that it didn't happen.

A thread of words.

She texted her husband - 11.40 train home. No reply.

Her dad was at breakfast, lost in thought, reading the newspaper. Her mum was nowhere to be seen. *Mum not up?* Clara's dad replied that he'd take her some toast later, which she wouldn't eat. A dull sadness swept over Clara. They ate in silence, except for Harry banging the table, making a mess. Her dad picked toast from the floor, tutted.

When Clara bustled away to catch her train, gathering coats, and toys, unfolding the pushchair, her dad barely raised his eyes from his paper.

Jay 2015

All the lads had been assembled in the club meeting room. The chairs, usually stacked against the walls or placed around the function tables, adorned with bows or laid with those white wedding covers, were bare and placed in rows before the projector screen. The lads almost never came up here - it was a huge room with a bar at one side and windows overlooking the car park on the other.

Posters for a'Spice Girls Tribute Night' were ranged in places at eye height along the walls. The plasma screen TV in the corner showed five second adverts for 'Comedy Night', 'Soccer School - under 12s' and 'Host your Office Christmas Party here!' Jay counted how long each advert was displayed for - five seconds each. Yes, five seconds, then the next and the next. Looping on and on.

No one sat next to each other, one seat apart mostly. Knees wide. Most of the guys slumped, heads bowed, looking at their phones. Four lads at the end, the young ones, bantered about something Jay couldn't catch. All of the boys shuffled.

Felt too much like school.

Steve came in. Opened the MacBook at the front and began logging in. They watched the screen before them come to life. Watched Steve's arrow move around the screen. PowerPoint - open recent - online life.

Right lads. Different kind of training today. I'll need you all watching cos this is important.

Phones went into pockets. Arms crossed. Jay lowered his body in the seat - pulled his cap down a bit.

Online safety. I don't want to patronise you right. I know you know this stuff. But we've got to go through it. All companies are doing this now right. Just to protect you and the club. Tick some boxes.

Steve laughed. One sound emitted. Embarrassed.

Right, firstly you are professionals so we have to make sure you only have official accounts on-line. No personal ones right. So they need to be deleted. Or under a pseudonym - you know like a fake name. Select who you allow to follow you carefully. Family, close friends, you know. Don't say anything controversial - like politics, or racist or sexist or whatever. I mean I know you wouldn't right. But big players have got into trouble for saying, you know, they support this political party or that one. Can be seen as coercive - you know, like you are telling people how to vote or whatever. Best stay out of all that.

There were slides about what is allowed - charity, anti-racism, anti-homophobia, saying happy birthday to your parents and all that. Part of Jay remembered he should delete his Facebook profile; part of him felt restless, numbed out, bored.

Steve went through security settings. He looked like he was boring himself.

Right, keep your sex life off your phones. Seriously. Everything has a digital fingerprint. It can be searched and traced. I can't tell you how to live your life. But you've been briefed before on drinking, gambling, dating - you know just be careful is what I'm saying. No cock shots lads - ha, ha! No seriously. You know, we can all name very high-profile players who have been in the press for their sex lives. We don't want that here. We ain't got the money the bigger clubs have for super-injunctions- ha, ha! No but seriously. Be careful, that's what we're saying here.

Someone said, 'Yeah Jonesy. Stop sexting my mum!' Everyone laughed.

Alright guys. Thanks for your time. You are free to go.

Jay thought of the time he'd seen another woman pop up on Steve's phone. That was probably nothing though. Nice guy. Too boring to have an affair or whatever. Clara had shot into his mind. But they hadn't spoken for months - was it a year? Fucking stupid he'd not been more careful. All deleted now. No one would care anyway. She wasn't the only one. But the others didn't matter. Never thought about them. None of it mattered.

Jay was straight out the door after the meeting. Across the car park. Key in pocket. Auto intuitive door unlock on his new four by four. He fucking loved this new car.

Over ninety on the A roads – heading back home for a couple of days. He had good news for his dad. Liam was coming home too. Proper family time.

Always the same greeting. He came in, using the same key he'd always had to the same front door. Flung his bag down in the narrow hallway, perhaps to indicate his arrival, as the white plastic door closed behind him. Mum would come through from the dining room or the garden, often half way to being drunk by then. He'd smell it in her skin as she lunged in for a hug, pretending surprise. *Jay! You're here!* And he felt her relief that he had come.

Dad would emerge, usually from upstairs or from the garage. *Good to see ya lad*. And would squeeze his arm or nudge him. Sometimes make a comment like, *nice to see you dressed up*, if Jay was in his trackies or his cap. Dad would take him off then to talk about the club, the games, the other games in the other leagues, who left, who stayed, who needed to go. Mum would dip in and out between drinks she hid or sipped from the can in the fridge.

How's Molly?
We split up mum. I told ya.

Did you? Why?

She was too clingy you know. Bit controlling. He couldn't tell her the truth.

Dad said, *Not surprised lad! She needed to keep you in check!*

Ha. Yeah well I just wanna be single a bit, you know. Can't be bothered.

Be careful who you are with though lad. You know some of them just want your money.

Mum said, *You'll meet someone Jay.*

Honestly mum, I'm not bothered at the moment.

Molly had pretty much fucked it for him anyway – telling her friends he was a cheat, wanted a MILF, that he was desperate. Showed them screen shots. Lucky he'd lied about who Clara was. Couldn't let it get back here though, back to home. Didn't want anyone else hurt. No point. And it wasn't even worth it. He hadn't seen Clara or done anything with her anyway. Just fantasy.

He could have told his mates that Molly had never let him go out after they moved in together, that she had been jealous of everyone, had followed his every move, quizzed him, cried and said she'd kill herself if he left. Once had hid his car keys so he had missed training. But he never told anyone. She had told him his friends were not good for him. Tried to stop him seeing his parents – refused to come with him home. Slagged off his brother – called him a fucking boring geek who thinks he's better than you. And that was for years, years. Well before Jay ever started texting other women.

At first Molly was charming, nice, comforting. Attentive.

Then it got weird; felt weird. Made him angry.

He was glad he got found out. Relieved she left. Ignored her begging him to take her back. Saying she'd forgive him. Then all the respect was gone. Changed his number.

He hoped so hard she had deleted those messages. He was hitting the big time now. No place for rumours or secrets.

Jay was glad to see Liam when he arrived home. He'd caught the bus even though Dad and Jay had offered to pick him up from the station. He didn't have a key. Had to knock. When he came in and hardly through the door, Jay hugged him, pulled his head down under the crook of his arm, rubbed his curly hair. Hugged him again. *Fuckin missed you mate. Love you bro. How's life? Listen mate, got something to tell ya. Might be movin up your way.*

Why? You getting a transfer?

Shhh. Might be. Keep it to y-self for now right. I'll tell the olds in a bit.

Alright. You okay, about Mol and all that?

Yeah. Pretty glad to tell you the truth. She was psycho. Good timing probably.

Mum greeted Liam like a child, stroking his face, too close to him with her own face. She seemed to peer at him like something she'd lost and then rediscovered like she was seeing him just born. But he did feel different to them. Further and further from the life they'd known in this house. Jay was drawn to his brother – he had something he wanted – but he didn't know what it was. Maybe distance from dad, from the pressure, from 'you should you shouldn't' – maybe that was it.

Dad stood back. Beckoned from the dining room. *Come in then lads. Let's eat.*

Over dinner Jay was watching. He saw his mum's heavy, drunk eyes. The effort of providing a meal, done, so she began to switch off. In the past he'd seen her fall asleep at the table - dad waking her, commanding her to *piss off and go to bed.* Tonight she rallied herself, even drank water at the table. Dad talked and talked, joking as ever, but these days avoiding the jokes that were at Liam's expense. In the past they had never gone a day it seemed without Liam being ridiculed in some way for Dad's amusement.

Liam told them about uni. Going well, he said. Learning about chemical engineering, using polymer composites. They pretended to understand some of it. He explained about planes being made from them, space craft, aeronautical something he called it. And how some future technologies were held back by the big oil companies because if they were used, the big guys would go out of business.

Don't suppose you approve of my new car then bro?

It looks nice mate. But you know I'm not into all that. If I was, I'd have that one though.

Your bike nearly cost as much.

Carbon Fibre frame. Light as a feather. Gotta lock it up right tho.

Hopefully be seeing it soon bro.

Go on they Jay - tell em.

Jay cleared his throat. Looked at the plate in front of him. Looked up at Dad then. Told them, he was going on loan to Sheffield. Massive co-incidence. But the idea is to get his name out there, get seen, get sold to one of the big clubs. A big move for him. Next step to the top.

Dad stood straight up. Like a fan cheering from the crowd, he lifted his arms and his face towards the ceiling. *Oh lad. I'm so proud of you. Finally. Knew you'd do it. Oh I can't wait to tell the guys. And your uncle Pete. Hey Jan, what do you think? Our boy's made it!*

Not quite yet dad. Nothing's signed. Anyway it's a step. Just a step.

Mum nodded. Smiled. *Glad you'll be able to look out for Liam.*

Jan! He's moving clubs. To get into the big time.

It's okay mum. I'll look out for our kid. He'll probably have to look out for me hey bro?

Liam just shook Jay's hand, hugged him, said *well done Jay,* warmly and honestly.

That night Jay told everything to Liam once his parents had gone to bed. They sat in his room like when they were kids. One on each end, pillow behind their backs, left legs out, right leg bent - they'd always done that.

Jay told his brother all about Molly and about Clara, and about what had been said between them but never done.

Liam was quiet. Kind. Listening. He said he wasn't surprised - knew Jay had liked Miss at school. He'd thought it was a crush. Joked - of course she fancied him - he was hot. Playfully nudged him.

But Jay was serious. Not laughing back.

Liam said, *I guess it's not as simple as that though is it? You can't choose who you happen to like. Good job nothing has happened though mate. You couldn't risk it. Not for either of you.*

Nah, it's all just talk bro. Anyway, I'm over that shit now.

Liam said he couldn't wait to get back to uni. Hated this house. Hated this fucking town.

So what shall I buy you once I'm minted then bro?

Ha. Nothing mate. I don't like all that stuff like you. It's all just bling. Just rubbish.

To you maybe. Dad'll be over the fucking moon when I buy them a new house.

That's the problem Jay. It's all about dad and what he wants. It fucking pisses me off. That's why I don't give a crap about all that shit. All that stuff. The watches and the houses and the cars and the haircuts. It's all just trying to look like you've got money. I'm proud I'm from a piss poor family. Don't give a shit that grandad was a failed rugby player as dad says. Least he worked hard - London dock worker. What's prouder than that? Fucking annoys me how much you care about what dad thinks.

Alright bro. It's alright. Anyway it's what everyone wants these days.

It's just images Jay. Pictures. In the paper, the TV, on the internet. That's a disaster waiting to happen. It's all surface. A screen. None of it is real.

Fuck off mate. Football is real. It's my job. I ain't slagging off your uni thing am I? I wouldn't wanna be reading all day. Doing chemical equations. But I ain't dissing you am I mate?

I ain't dissing you. I just hope you are doing all this for a good reason. That you want to. Cos you might be empty at the end.

What does that mean?

You already lost some of your - spark, I guess. You seem more and more like those lads on tv, after the matches you know, interviewed but just say the same old shit. I'm not saying you are like that. But you are less, I dunno, alive. I just don't want you to lose yourself.

I won't mate.

And maybe this Miss Horton thing. Maybe it's meant to be. Like if it feels so magnetic, like you said, like it feels when you talk about it. Like maybe you have to choose.

I choose football bro. That's my life. That other stuff is just a game. A fantasy. Can take it or leave it mate, you know.

Jay knew now, lying in his childhood bed, that football was all he wanted. He knew it was a ticking clock. Each time he got injured he felt the push of time - knew it wasn't a forever job. But it was all he wanted right now. All he wanted.

But it was always Clara there, waiting in the crowd, just as he floated on the ebb of sleep.

Clara 2016

Sat on the other side of the Headteacher's desk, laid with two bottles of unopened water and a small plate of Custard Creams, Clara barely took a breath before answering his question.

I recognise the changing cohort here and I feel that our priorities as a school need to be closing the gap, especially in regard to the lower levels of literacy we are seeing as students come to us from our feeder schools. Work needs to be done there in terms of our incoming students from Year 6. We also should recognise the need to support our intake from lower income families and our increasing concerns around safeguarding which is seriously impacting the time and workload of our pastoral team.

And how do you see us moving forward in that regard? asked the Headteacher, his pen now down and his eyes meeting hers.

It's a simple equation. Re-evaluating the budget so that money is focused on recruitment, in order to increase staff numbers, thereby allowing more time for those staff who need more time to have more time.

This takes consideration and planning, but I have that planning and costing here if you'd like to take a look.

He looked over Clara's planning - raised his eye brows, and then looked again at her.

In addition, we need to consider the new requirements of the examining boards and the curriculum which continues to become more challenging. Heads of Department need time to plan effectively for this. Frankly, the curriculum is less focused on creative arts and sport and more on traditionally literacy heavy subjects. This makes focusing on literacy even more important. The second page covers that. Just there.

Here she laid out, along with her ideas for getting their staff into primary schools to make the transition between primary and secondary smoother, her plans for removing the sports accolades from the walls of the school and replacing them with large quotes from the key texts for English Literature and with the mathematical rules required for the GCSE.

Hmmm. I'm not sure about that Clara. It is important to give our students role models. Some of our sports students do very well.

Yes. Agreed. But keep it over in the sports block or in reception if needed. What we need these days is students who are able to quote from a book, not those who are only able to run fast or kick a ball. I'm not saying that's right. It's just how it is.

After a further twenty minutes or more of this - of Clara being entirely in command, though her head rushed and her body ran with the buzz of adrenaline, the Head shook her hand and thanked her.

Returning to the staff room, her chest seemed to expand beyond its bounds.

Her long-known colleagues passed her on their way to the pigeon holes or the coffee machine, as she sat legs crossed, hands crossed, pushing her right nails over and over into her left hand. They asked her how it was going, telling her what they thought of her rival candidates. She felt things would change between them, felt they already had.

Fraser never changed. Came and sat down next to her. Crossed his arms. Stretched his long legs before him, one over the other at the ankles. *So?* He said.

Yep. It's okay I think. I said everything I'd planned in the interview. Just have to see.

He reached into his top pocket. Handed her a chocolate bar. *Drink later?*

I'm tired. Gotta get back. I'll text you later what they decide.

You're a machine these days Clara. Careful.

I'm fine. I can do all this. That's what nursery is for. Anyway, people have to work. It's good for sons to see their mothers working.

He patted her leg. *Okay then. Good luck. If you want it.*

As she walked through reception on her way to the car, she saw, as she did every day, the framed signed shirt - Benson 11. That'll be the first thing I take down, she thought.

Four weeks later, all sports memorabilia and photos, all 'alumni' pictures and trophies were removed. They had been taken to the sports block where she never went. EB12 had become the room the trainee teachers always had, so she never had to go there either. Now she had her own office, with a door plaque - Mrs C Horton Deputy Headteacher. She dropped her child at nursery as it opened and collected him as it closed, every day. She bathed him, read to him, put him to bed, cooked, worked, slept on the sofa, dragged herself to bed. And began again the same way each day.

She began to dread the weekends.

Work was easier. She knew her role, her place. She had command. She had a plan.

At home nothing was easy. When she drove into her cul-du-sac and saw the shrubs in the driveway in need of pruning, when she saw the 1930s frontage which had drawn her to this house in need of repainting, when she saw the cracks in the front door in need of replacing, and when she opened the door to her broken marriage and skirted around the issues and cursed the fridge left open and the flower beds needing weeding, she felt exhausted. The weight of all the fixing that needed to be done.

But we are superhuman - perfect mothers, perfect managers and leaders, we look good, sound good, work hard, socialise, are wives, partners, friends, colleagues. We are the epitome of modern woman.

Underneath we are loosely tacked together - coming apart at the seams, unravelling. The moths are doing their work.

One Saturday, six months ago, Clara had been sending a parcel at the post office. Got there just before it closed. Her mother's birthday present. A cushion with her son's face on it. Would never get used no doubt. Didn't match her mother's floral decor. Wouldn't suit the new suite. Anyway it was already six days late. A man in front of her in the queue was reading a tabloid. She saw Jay on the back - jogging with some other footballers she vaguely recognised – 'Benson New Signing' the headline said. Perhaps once she would have felt proud. Her stomach moved, turned, she felt sick. There was a swallowing. She breathed hard. Pushed it out, under, away.

After the parcel was sent she bought the paper. Didn't read it.

It was a cold day. About eight degrees. She got home, filled the coal scuttle, used the back page of the paper first to light their fire in the living room.

Easter term staff night out. The kind of thing Clara avoided these days. The discomfort of being the boss. No one ever acted themselves around her these days. The uncomfortable silences, the whispers, the fact she felt she had to buy everyone a drink. *I don't give a fuck. Get as drunk as you like. Say what you want. I'm not going to shop you to the boss. Tell me what you think of me and I'll tell you what I think of you.* Last time she had gone out, she'd bought everyone shots and ended up singing karaoke whilst some trainee Maths teacher tried to touch her arse. Probably a dare. Fuck - that was a mistake. Apparently the staff 'loved it', she was 'human for once'.

She was a human - just not one they were allowed to see.

She'd never let that happen again.

Fraser met her at the usual end of term teacher pub in town. They arrived early. Only the government-initiative-training-programme teachers were there before them - overdressed, over tanned and two bottles of Prosecco down. Clara and Fraser sat deep in a corner, outside. He offered her a cigarette. She glanced over to the newbies and then thought fuck it. Human. Fraser told her he was going to try to pull the blonde one tonight. *They are all blonde Fraser. Which one?*

The blonde one. There. Alison.

Aneka.

Yeah Aneka. Science?

Probably.

Look over there. Is that Charlotte something? There Clara. That girl with the black dress - short one. There? Remember her.

Oh yeah. Maybe. Think I taught her in Year 8 or something.

Is she fair game? In her 20s now.

Ha! Course. Go on Fraser. I'd like to see you try.

Clara went in to the bar. Offered a drink to the newbies on the way. Bought them more Prosecco. A bottle for herself and a pint for Fraser. Sat back at the table.

Alone. That jangling feeling. Need to take out the mobile. Scroll it for nothing. Just to feel connected.

Alone.

Clara downed one glass of Prosecco. Was shuffling over the bench to move close to the newbies as they fell into one another's naked shoulders.

Clara felt an arm around her neck - *I'm being mugged.* A huge body fell into her, a clamouring body. Calm, accepting that she was about to be hurt, against her control. She looked into his face. *Miiiiiiisss! Fuck! What you doin here? You don't look no different! Remember me don't ya? I was a fuckin nightmare in your classes.*

She did remember him. As a boy. Now a fully grown man - two full sleeve tattoos and a beard. His name was Chris, or Kane, or Craig. *How are you doing Craig? What you up to these days?*

I was inside for bit. Now I'm runnin my uncle's club with him. Bouncer most nights. You still teaching? You was my favourite teacher. Fuckin gutted I forgot to do that English exam.

Now it came back to her. Craig was a traveller kid. Dad in prison. Worked hard in her lessons. Could have got a B. Scraped a C. Got off his face the night before his second exam. Forgot to turn up. Arrested for ABH - beat up a bloke in the street outside his girlfriend's house. Those were the days before Clara bothered filling in pink pieces of paper for safeguarding on every story a kid ever told her. Heard he had gone inside.

But in this light, in his face, in the eyes that were his child eyes, he looked soft and vulnerable like he had to her many times.

Fraser came over. Touched her arm. *Sorry to interrupt. Think we need to get out of here Clara. Need to talk.*

What have you done Fraser? Ha. Bye Craig. Nice to see you.

Fraser took her arm below the wrist, firmly, pulled her away from the table. She hadn't known him like this before. Great urgency. He walked ahead of her, glancing back, right through the pub to the front entrance. Onto the street.

Shit Clara. You have fucked this up.

He walked on through town until they came to a smaller pub. One she'd never been in before. It was empty and smelled of spilled beer and bleach. He sat in a dark corner.

Shouldn't we buy a drink?

Go on then. I'll wait here. He was angry or something.

Clara bought the same round again. Downed a glass of Prosecco at the bar and went back to sit with Fraser. Slid his pint to him.

What's going on Fraser?

God I hope this is not true Clara.

What?

That girl Charlotte. She used to go to our school. She knew you. I never taught her but you taught her boyfriend in Year 11. Years ago.

Clara knew what was coming. Her stomach felt it, tighter, closing her lungs from the bottom.

That Charlotte girl just told me that she'd heard that you had an 'inappropriate' relationship with that boy. The one she went out with. Is it true?

What? No! With who? What is she talking about?

She was ready to have it out with you right there. That would have been a disaster for you. True or not. She was angry and drunk. Ready to lynch you.

Well that's rubbish.

There are screen shots apparently of you having a conversation - a dirty one - with him. Benson. He was trouble Clara.

What?

Clara suddenly became aware of the whole world tilting. A haze spread over her vision. Like a filter on a screen. A dull sickness came over her.

Everything every-day a minute ago was odd, unreal, no longer attached.

She was staring. Very quiet.

What happened Clara? Fraser was softer now.

It was nothing. Just a few silly messages. It was fantasy. He started the whole thing.

When? How old was he?

Nineteen. An adult. Nothing happened. It's all over now.

You have to be careful. You're a senior member of staff. You have a family. When did you last talk to him?

Oh over a year ago. Forget it. I have. It was silly.

So this went on for what…three years or something? That sounds like it's more than nothing.

Look. My flirtations with a grown adult are no concern of the school. It's done with anyway.

Fraser looked at Clara for a long time. She looked down at her drink. At her hands.

She really wanted then to be home, to be in bed, to not be here.

Clara, don't worry. I've got your back. That Charlotte girl is probably jealous or trying to make trouble. Maybe he was bragging about it or something. That's what these lads can be like.

In a future time, recalling this in therapy, Clara would come to know the shame - the shame of suddenly feeling used, something to brag about; the shame of knowing that other people knew, that somewhere her words of real desire had been read; the shame of feeling humiliated. The shame that it could hurt, ruin, break her world and all she was expected to be.

And the loss, the knowing it was over.

And the knowing that this, this world, this place, this life was all she was ever going to have - and how empty that felt.

Clara lay in bed that night. Her husband in the spare room so she 'wouldn't wake him' when she came in, he had said. Her heart pushed the blood, adrenaline, alcohol so hard around her body that it seemed to move the whole of her - like a plastic cup thrown back and forth on a wave -never stilling, never quite reaching the shore.

Thinking. Thinking of all the permeations of what could happen. Panic rising - ebbing up, up. What had she done wrong: professionally, personally, morally? Why had he bragged, betrayed? How did that girl know? Who else knew?

Why did anyone care?

And because she felt like the panic would kill her. And because she needed sleep. And because it was far, far out of her control; she decided she would be honest. Just honest. If all she had done, and really because she had done nothing, she would be honest.

If anyone ever cared about a two-bit teacher and a generic, identikit, footballer.

Why would they? No one would.

Clara 2017

Clara's mother had died. Died. Just like that.

Her father had texted one afternoon. It was a Thursday. Clara was at a golf club undergoing management training. During the session on 'personality styles', while her mind drifted to a holiday she had once had in France with her cousins, when she had held an electric fence for too long, her phone flashed.

Mum is in hospital. Had a fall. Nothing to worry about.

Clearly something to worry about.

She thought of her father there. Alone.

Dad, I'm coming home on the next train.

She thought, if it is nothing he will protest.

Thank you darling.

He had never called her that.

So she rang her husband. Explained what she knew. Said their son needed picking up from nursery. Of course she'd be gone all weekend. Yes you will have to take a day off. Well that's what happens when there is an emergency. She could not read this in him - this strange anger, this strange resentment.

The journey up north was long. Many changes at stations further and further into the coldness. She listened to some playlist on Spotify that filled an emotional need - 90s hits. She cried. This was an odd grief for something not yet real. Clara feared, above all, a life of servitude having to take care of her mother who had never been able to take care of her. Or worse, taking care of her father who would give up his writing to take care of her belligerent mother, whilst she also took care of her son and her husband and her school. Suddenly the sky buckled and warped around her and her stomach caved in.

And she cried at the unbearable weight of all that.

She went straight to the hospital by taxi from the station. It was strange. The hospital was sprawling. It had a Marks & Spencer, and Starbucks and other commercial outlets that made it feel like a shopping centre. And the walls muted any noise. And the ward was half empty. But felt hot and impersonal and smelled of death.

Death is a smell. It is sharp. It has an earthy sweetness. It is pervading. It is primitive.

Later, Clara had tried to describe this smell to her husband - but, like the grindings and pulsing and pain of childbirth, she had no way to make him know this, as it had gone from her, despite the human intensity with which she'd experienced both birth and death.

She looked at her mother. Fed with a tube up her nose. Small in the bed. Grey. Sunken. She was asleep the whole time Clara was there. Clara was glad.

She had nothing to say to her.

The doctor took Clara into a room and asked about resuscitation. Yes her mother would want this. It strangled her to say it. The doctor told her that mother had basically starved herself. The doctor asked whether her mother had a history of anorexia or other eating disorders.

Yes. Mum didn't eat really. She loved those cookery shows you know? She'd watch hours of cooking shows. And she had a massive collection of expensive pots and pans and knives and things you honestly wouldn't even know what they were for. But she never cooked. Crazy really. She was obsessed with her weight. I remember as a child she would have weight graphs she filled in and fridge magnets, you know, a moment on the lips is a lifetime on the hips. God. I mean. How can the body sustain that? No fuel. For years.

And the doctor said, softly, with a knowing: *It can't Clara.*

I don't even know when I last saw her eat. I saw her eat a prawn a couple of years ago when we went out for dinner. Last month, Christmas, she didn't eat a thing. Just drank fizzy water. She could hardly walk then. I guess I knew this was the end - then - I knew.

Returning to her bedside, she saw her mother awake. Just. It was hard to find the kindness required in that moment to do what, comfort her? Did her mum even know she was dying? The doctor had said she would do what she could. They would do what they could. The plan was to feed her through this tube until she was strong enough to take soup or solid foods. She had come to them dehydrated - this was almost under control now, she said.

She looked so old there so frail her skin thin the blue veins like worms under there her hands swollen her face sinking her teeth yellow brown the bed too big so short so broken her hair grey under the dye the roots matting the pillows eating her head. no mother. a child. tiny tiny tiny in the bed. The beep beep of the machines and the worrying sound now and then they made and the way she jumped each time and looked at Clara in panic and the sinking away again of her breath and the smells of food and sick and shit that seemed stuck to the ceiling waiting to drop.

She sat right next to the bed, took her mum's hand. It was elegant. Long fingers. Nails painted. Post box red, as ever. The chips not obvious from a distance. She hoped her mother would squeeze her hand. Like they do in films. But instead she pulled it away and began to pull at the tube in her nose.

No mum. You can't take that out. It's keeping you alive. I know it hurts. It must be sore. I know. I'm sorry mum. It's not forever. Just until you are stronger.

Clara wished her dad would come back. She felt unbearable. Later she would know this was guilt, resentment, fear, self-preservation, resistance, and overwhelming love which she had not allowed herself to feel ever for this woman whom she had not ever known as a mother.

That holiday to France, the one with the cousins, that summer her mother had been happy. That was the only time she remembered her as a real mother, tender, happy, laughing. She had seen in the memories of that summer, her mum, sitting at a long white painted wooden table outside a French farmhouse with huge shutters overlooking an orchard, opening onto a patio dappled with sunlight between apple tree leaves.

Her mother ate cheeses and pâtés and bread and drank red wine and looked elegant and happy and content and hugged her and called her beautiful and stroked her hair and laughed when she came back from the river having held the electric fence too long, but had comforted her. And she knew her mother smiling at a man who was her colleague with whom they were holidaying and dad writing all day in a room with white curtains and never coming into the sun.

A wildness ebbed from her mother then, and from Clara, a knowing of all things and all feelings and no cages or doors or binding. rivers. trees. flowers. rain in the air. the smell of moss and of tree bark.

Back in the city, once home, all the peace, contentment, motherly-love was gone and the familiar dread and pain and distance returned. And her mother's nails were painted again. She left her job after that holiday. Clara never knew why. She didn't work again. And fell into cookery shows and diet books.

Her mother said then from her hospital bed, very faintly, a whisper: *Where's you father? Is Harry here? Don't bring little Harry here. I don't want him to see me like this. Go and get your father.*

Clara got up then. Left the room. Walked from the ward. Stood in the long, empty corridor with the coloured lines painted on the floor.

Cried.

Round a corner, almost hidden, she saw her dad, drinking coffee from a Starbucks cup and staring out of the window. She knew then that he couldn't do this either. That it was hard for him. Maybe he felt the guilt. She thought he should. Somehow it all, all of it, felt like his fault. He should have stopped this, saved them both.

That night, once Clara and her dad were home, in the night, the house phone rang. Her father answered it. Roused from a dream in which a man had broken into her car and was waiting in the back seat, Clara found her father putting on his shoes in the dark hallway. Her heart still beat fast from the dream. He said he was going to the hospital - mum had had a stroke in the night. They thought he should come, now. Clara knew what it meant. Her father didn't seem to. On the way to the hospital he still spoke of how he would take care of her if she was unable to get around the house - beds downstairs and all that.

But Clara knew it was the end.

When they arrived, she had been moved to ICU. A further stroke had hit her hard and her internal organs were struggling. Clara's father went straight in and sat by the bed. Clara couldn't. She couldn't. She sat in the waiting area with the other families. Perhaps it was one family. A teenager, one of their family members, was dying. Injuries from a motorbike accident.

Somehow she could bear this sadness, someone else's sadness, but not her own.

At 8.16 am, her mother died. Died. Just like that. A nurse came and told Clara. Put her in a special room. It had a box of half sized, functional, hospital tissues and a glass table with magazines on it.

She was alone. That was the most alone she had ever felt.

Alone.

She knew then that there really only was her, on the planet. Only her.

Never more alone.

She and her dad went back home. To the family home where Clara had grown up. The home that had not been home.

It was suburban, mock-Tudor, standard, 80s kitsch, diamond leaded windows in UPVC, white conservatory with the condensation that sits in old double-glazing, neat, bland, boring. Except for her father's study which was upstairs and faced the garden. That was brimming over with book cases and seven old typewriters he had collected, one with a European keyboard she had loved as a child, not 'querty'.

And photos and photos and photos in boxes and frames and Blu-tacked to the walls of family on every side, some of whom Clara had never met.

And little balls of paper everywhere, mostly near the wicker basket bin which he used as a target when he had writer's block. It seemed that may have been common recently, or else the balls had not been picked up.

In the living room, by the gas coal fire, her dad read the paper. Clara had found some old photos of her grandparents from the study boxes - she looked through them remembering her grandmother, mother's mum, whom she had adored.

Clara and her dad watched old tv comedies of his choosing. There was a relief - they were happier together than before. Clara kept expecting her mother to appear through the living room door asking what they were talking about, not wanting to miss out. Accusingly, but never with genuine interest.

Why didn't you want to sit with mum?
I couldn't dad. I had nothing to say.
It was hard wasn't it?
Was he talking about her death or her life?
Yes. More than I could bear.

She realised then that she wanted to see her mother - dead. The body. Like that would allow her to accept that she was really gone. Really dead.

Dad, I'm going to see the body. Tomorrow.
Good idea darling. We'll go up there together, I need to get the death certificate sorted out.

Her father sat that evening in the room next to her old bedroom, and she heard, as she had many times before, the tap of the keyboard, softer now it was a laptop than the old days past of the typewriter and then the PC. But she heard him flowing with ideas, driving the story out, rarely hesitating.

The block was gone.

Clara was led into the very depths of the hospital. The part hidden, unseen. Like an underground road system, punctuated with industrial doors that lead to departments and storage areas. A guy in chef's whites leaned against a yellow bin on wheels, smoking and scrolling his phone. Further along, and into the darkness, an empty trolley was wheeled into a lift by a porter. Clara and the woman from the morgue ascended through a fire door, along another empty corridor and Clara was asked to wait.

Sorry to keep you waiting love. We have had a major this week. We're busy down here. Won't keep you.

A major? Incident? Perhaps the motorbike crash or a pile-up she'd missed on the news. She hadn't seen real news for days. Time changes after a death.

Clara was nervous.

An interior door opened and the morgue lady asked her to come in. A small room. More functional half-sized tissues. A vase of fake lilies.

When you are ready, go through the door. Your mum is in there. I will wait outside.

Clara went though.

Her mother was laid out, covered in a sheet. Naked under there she guessed. Her hands and arms outside the sheet. Her face still. Her eyes closed, one a little open. Her body didn't look alive. It looked dead. Nothing she'd been told about them looking asleep was true. She looked dead - and that was all.

I don't want to touch you mum. I'm sorry. She began like that. And then the words gushed from her. She told her she loved her. She forgave her. She understood. And the rest, later when trying to recall, she could not remember. But it came from her like all she had ever wanted to say. And then *goodbye mum.*

Clara went back though the door. Was taken back to the front door, or the side door, there were so many entrances to this place. And she stood, waiting for her dad, thinking about paying for the parking at the machine behind her.

The molten lava of tears were heavy in her chest. Didn't come though. The word was 'bereft' - bereft of everything: of feeling, of love, of a mother, of a life she'd wanted but never had.

Miss Horton?

Clara turned around. She wasn't sure who had said it, or even if it had been said. Then she saw a man looking at her - she felt him before she really registered him properly.

Standing by the drinks machine was Jay.

What are you doing here?

Jay. Good to see you.

You too.

My mum died. Here. She...well I had to come and...well I came to…

Oh my god. I'm sorry.

God, he looked amazing.

A man.

Like the photos she'd seen, but a breathing, moving body that pulled at her. Tightened about her. He smiled and ran his hand though his hair.

What are you doing here? Long way from home.

Had a match here yesterday. Had a fall, you know, on the pitch. My ankle went over, again. Just been discharged. Tests and checks, you know. To see if it's torn again.

And is it?

No. It's fine. Just, you know, not that strong from all the past injuries. But I'm ok. Back to physio. Probably have to have a few weeks not playing matches. It'll be ok.

You going back today then?

No. Got a hotel tonight. Heading back tomorrow. Taxi on its way. Are you going back?

Home? No. Got a couple more nights here till dad and I get some formalities settled. I'll head back Monday morning I guess.

Jay's face had changed. He was looking at her now whereas before his eyes were elsewhere, beyond her, next to her. He looked at her, like he always used to, right into her eyes. They both paused there. A growing sense of a lifting began in her chest.

Jay said, *come back with me now?*

She was in resignation mother dead everything dead nothing to fear or know or understand just that moment where nothing was real and no one was watching.//
The time was right. It had never been more right.//
Destiny, the universe, whatever - had decided that this would come to pass.//
Now in this moment.//
Nothing else existed except she and Jay.

Yes.

Clara took out her phone. Texted: *Dad I've bumped into a friend. Head back without me. See you later.*

The taxi pulled up. Clara and Jay didn't speak. They were silent together across the city. He slid his hand over her leg.

They did all they had fantasised about. Talked about.
And they talked that night - but somehow couldn't say anything that answered the questions about why this hadn't happened before and why it seemed to mean so much and why their lives had moved together and apart so many times.

Jay 2017

Nearly two years he'd lived here now - in a flat of his own, over-looking the city (sort of, if you looked hard into the distance). The skyline of Manchester could be beautiful at night, when the vast sprawl of lights were scattered over the city.

Below his window was a car park, and beyond that more apartment blocks made from urban grey brick and one-way, mirrored, blacked out windows. At night the apartments became almost invisible. But by day their mirrored glass reflected the River Irwell. On bright spring days, when the river glinted, the sparkle ran ripples over the mirrored glass. Jay loved those days - although his days out were long, and he was often away, and so the rare mornings spent watching the rippling glass were precious.

He shared the flat now with Dina. He had met her through a team-mate. It had been last winter, the dead of the season, heavy with games and with excitement. The club had started well and they were out celebrating, pretty low-key, at a bar in the city. Just some of the lads there, the ones without families, babies, mostly. No-one was drinking.

From a table they had on a balcony, away from the bustle below, Jay spotted his mate's girlfriend. *Hey Stan, ain't that your Missus?* They had glared over the balcony and jeered at her. Good natured. Stan had shouted *Come up Stevie - meet these losers!*

Stevie was one of those girls, kind of made-in-a-factory, plastic. Long dark hair, curly. Make-up, so much she looked like it had been sprayed on. Maybe it had. Some girls did that. She looked inhuman, doll like. But she was nice, very softly spoken, very tame, very - maybe - shy. It was hard to tell. And she didn't smile really. Jay thought she was probably just not very clever, but had looks, and so he thought maybe that was what was interesting about her.

On the balcony with the boys, Jay felt almost sorry for her. They were teasing her, definitely teasing her: *what you doing out love? shouldn't you be at home warming the bed for Stan? you lookin to pull tonight Stevie, all dressed up? we're just kiddin lass, don't worry. drink? what you so serious for?* They gave up after a while - went back to their football chat.

Stevie sat next to Stan. She looked bored. She was texting someone, scrolling her phone. Then it rang. *Yeah I am in here Dee. I'm up in the VIP balcony. Come up. No seriously. Yeah they'll let you in. I'll tell em now.* She asked if they minded if her mate came up for a bit, not long, they were going on to somewhere else soon.

Dina struggled a little awkwardly up the stairs in her heels. There was no glamour about her walk, Jay thought. She was like Stevie - sprayed on beauty - but she had more life. More spark. *Alright lads?* she said. That was bold - friendly. She was blonde. She was cheeky. She came over and squeezed Jay's bum. Just like that. *Whoa - hang on love! What you do that for?* She smiled and said, *You're the only one standing up, so it was easy pickings.*

Dina leaned over the balcony with Jay. She pointed at people and talked about their clothing. Laughing. At one point she said, *Oh my god I went to school with her!* Jay thought she was funny, fun - but cheap, nothing charming, nothing mysterious about her. *Come on Stevie, let's get out of here. We're gonna miss Becky if we don't go now.*

And that was it. Dina took Stevie by the arm and dragged her off, throwing Stevie's fur collared coat over her arm and ungracefully clattering back down the spiral staircase.

Later that night, in the taxi home, Jay found her on Facebook. Friend requested her. She accepted his request at some point in the early hours of the morning. Jay was up early the next day, went for a jog, went to the gym. Didn't give Dina another thought.

In the days following though, they started chatting - messaging. He had a couple of evenings free that week - asked her if she wanted to meet.

Jay arrived first. He walked into the supper club which was filled around the perimeter with round tables, each with an old-fashioned table lamp in the middle. The bar itself was wrought iron and mirrored inside – it was surrounded by the tables. Above was a balcony running the whole perimeter of the building on which people held drinks and chatted. It was retro, vintage, classy, subtle, soft here. With dimmed lighting and 1930s music lolling along in the background.

He didn't remember ever taking another girl on a date.

Not Molly - psycho - who he'd met at the gym.

Not Charlotte - clingy - whom he'd been on and off with since school.

All the others, just one-night stands.

Clara was there with him for a second, two, three, turning to smile at him. Taking his arm. Leading him to a table.

Dina arrived then, came up, grabbed his bum again. *Alright Jay? Nice place. Bit quiet. I could never afford this.*

At the table, as they looked at the menu, Jay had a strange sensation. He felt watched. His body was moving without him - jittering - looking behind and above him. Dina asked the waiter what was a cep, what was a foam, what was an essence, what was a sweetbread, what was a crevette, what was a reduction.

Then he knew this feeling was embarrassment.

Dina talked, almost incessantly, about herself - her job as a call handler for a big law firm. How she liked dogs. Wanted a pug. Her family - her brother she worshipped, actually using that word.

Jay listened - gave up trying to interject. Instead he took her in, what was attractive about her. What wasn't. There was no softness, no melting, no part of her that was vulnerable. She was uncomplicated - brash, loud.

He looked at her dress when she got up to go to the toilet. It was one long cream-coloured tube and fitted her so that her boobs looked huge and so did her bum. When Dina returned and launched again into a story about her brother, how he should be a pro player, Jay zoned her out and thought about her under her dress.

It was better that way.

After dinner they went back to his flat. Had sex. It was okay. Did the job. She seemed to like it. He never knew if they did or not. Molly had told him once that he was shit in bed; that she pretty much always faked it. That he was selfish. Truth was, he didn't really know how not to be shit at sex, or care if he was. Women had sex with him and he mostly liked it. They wouldn't come back if he weren't no good - right? His dad had once said, *Lad, sex is just one big bloody disappointment.* Liam had rolled his eyes at that. Jay never knew why - never asked Liam that. But really dad was right.

He didn't really want to see Dina again. Wasn't that bothered.

But he did see her again. And again. Mostly at the flat, for sex and box sets and her drinking wine and him gambling on his phone and sometimes a walk along the river. Well once. And her talking and him listening. And him wondering how long this would last.

That was nearly a year ago.

He was ready to end it. Even the talking had stopped and most nights they would be silent. And she'd say, *What's up? Why haven't you got anything to say?*

God it was boring.

One day she came over to the flat. She was strange. She brushed straight past him, went to the toilet, didn't look him in the eye.

Jay had a sense something was wrong. His stomach sank. He waited. Sat on the sofa. Stared at the picture they had bought from Ikea - a magnified atom. He thought about atoms, how they are inside cells, how cells grow.

She stood in the doorway of the bathroom. The light was behind her. In her hand she held a white stick - at first he thought it was an e-cigarette - was about to ask why she was using it. He didn't like smoking or anything similar to it. She was looking at it. Held it up for him to see, except he couldn't see it from where he sat and where she stood.

What?

Look at it.

What is it?

It's a pregnancy test. It's gone pink.

Jay stood up, went over, took it, looked at the pink in the middle. It didn't mean anything to him. But he felt an awful dread.

What does it mean?

I'm pregnant.

Jay gave it back to her. Went back to the sofa. Sat. Head in hands. For a while he watched a cobweb gently drifting back and forth between the corners of the coffee table.

Everything he had known to be real a moment ago was no longer real. The world tilted. He thought, is this how Clara had felt when she found out she was pregnant? This panic. This is fucking awful.

His father's words came into his head. Family first. Always family first.

I don't think we can have a baby now Dee.

Well we are having one.

Yeah but we need to think about this. It's a cell. We don't have to have it.

I want to have it. I've been thinking about it. I thought I was pregnant and I've thought about it. I think we should keep it.

What about what I think?

Dee came over to him. Sat next to him. Put her hand on his leg. He was reassured - thought she'd be reasonable then. He looked at her, smiled.

I'm the mother so I get to decide.

Jay stood then. Paced to the wall opposite. Turned. His body felt tight. His chest too. His thumbs pressed into his palms.

I don't want it Dee. I can't be a dad.

Suddenly the walls were getting closer. The flat felt tiny.

He went to the door - started putting his trainers on.

Where are you going?

Just need to get out. Have a think.

You are upsetting me Jay.

Yeah well I'm upset. I've got to think.

He went out then, hearing Dina calling after him. He guessed this hadn't gone how she'd hoped. But he didn't want a baby, with her. He jogged down the three flights of stairs. Started jogging down the tow path. He felt his tight jeans against his knees, knew he looked strange running like this. Walked.

He didn't want this because he didn't love Dina. He didn't know himself. He wasn't ready.

He had a job that was bigger than this. Because he wanted to be free. Because a baby with her was the wrong mother. Because he saw the graffiti on the tow path edges, by the canal, and knew this world wasn't right for children. Because he didn't want to be a dad, his dad, he didn't want to be like his dad. Because he was free and he wanted to be free.

God.

Then he sat on a bench and the river still flowed past despite everything. He watched the litter caught in the edges. But he didn't see it. He thought about a baby, holding a baby, feeding a baby, showing a baby to his parents. It felt unreal, not like something that could happen.

Suddenly Jay felt tired. So tired. His head, which before had been sparking was still, his body melted into the bench. He felt nothing - at all - not one feeling and not one thought.

Just the litter floating down the river.

Jay returned to the flat. Took off his trainers. Went to the kitchen. Reached for a glass. Got some water from the tap. Drank it hurriedly. Thought about packing; he'd be away for four days now. Saw Dina still sat at the sofa, glaring as he had done at the cobweb under the table.

Dee. Have the baby if you want. I'll support you. We're both in on this - we both did it.

I want you to be happy Jay.

Yeah well I can't feel what I'm not. Give me time.

I'm going to my mam's. I'll maybe see you when you're back.

Yeah I'll call ya.

Dina got up. Left without looking at him.

Jay was sad he'd hurt her. She was expecting him to be more than he was.

People always say you are pregnant for nine months. In fact it is ten. Or close enough. Jay had been surprised to learn this.

A lot happens in ten months. They had won the league. He got another player award. They bought a baby seat for the car and a cot and a Moses basket and a monitor and pads for wee and for milk and tiny little clothes in 'new born' and smaller than that and nappies and cotton wool balls and blankets and books about babies and a buggy. They bought the most expensive items they could buy for baby maintenance. Jay had decided he wanted to look good in the photos in the paper as he pushed the baby in the park. He wanted to be like that royal couple proudly fixing the baby in the car seat for the first time, evoking tears from the MILFs reading it in *Hello.*

They'd been asked to do a photo shoot for some tabloid supplement online. And although a part of him knew Dina wanted it and his agent wanted it, he had said no. That embarrassment came again.

Dina folded nappies away in drawers and the little clothes. The buggy was parked awkwardly in the hallway.

All these things were real, but they were for someone else's baby.

Dina grew bigger, calmer.

Jay felt nothing. Sometimes an impression of dread came in the night. But he brushed it away and spat it down the sink each morning.

One night, Jay was sleeping in a hotel in Leicester. The baby wasn't due for another three weeks.

But his phone rang in the night - 2am - rang and rang until it finally stirred him.

The baby was coming. waters broken toilet pain close together mum came hospital go back home few hours codeine yoga ball breathing come home come home home. baby coming.

Something innate, urgent, came into Jay. He dressed quickly, stuffed clothes, phone, headphones into his bag. Texted the gaffer - *Baby's coming. Gotta go mate. Sorry.* Lift to the car park, hotel room keys in a metal box down there, start engine, drive home. Called Dina as soon as he was on the motorway - *on my way, it's ok, be there soon, keep breathing, best get to hospital, yes I think so, meet you there.*

He parked in the huge car park, shoving the barrier ticket in his back pocket. He remembered what they said about how long it can take and how boring it can be for the partner and how you might want to bring Netflix. So he went through the bag and grabbed his headphones.

Put them around his neck. Phone in back pocket. The sun was coming up. He thought about the press outside the maternity ward doors - realised he'd look a cunt with his headphones on, about to greet his baby; took them off, folded them. Hid them from view.

No press there though.

Then he thought - this is a family thing, a real thing, not press and plaudits and shakes of the hand. Just a woman giving birth to a baby. One that he had made. That was half him. That was going to be his own - family first. A real human thing - really truly human.

In the room where he found Dina, her mother was there holding her hand. When he arrived, she smiled at him and stepped aside. Dina was on all fours on a bed, in the corner of a private room, the midwife moving around checking things that Jay knew nothing of Mary, Dina's mum, said she'd leave them to it for now.

Then it was them alone. The midwife coming back in fifteen minutes. At first it seemed like nothing was happening - a false alarm. So calm and normal except for the strange position Dina was in. But then a contraction came and he was thrown into a new place. Dina's face contorted and she zoned away, pulled the mask to her face and breathed. Then it passed.

Jay was scared. And wanted this to stop. And the more contractions came, the more he felt not present, not there, not needed.

After a while he wondered when he should start watching Netflix.

But then it all came so suddenly. The midwife did a check, said it was time, told Dina to push, asked Jay to hold her hand, be where she could see him. Then there was talk about how it was good, and a head, and how well Dina was doing and not long now, shoulders. And then a cry.

And a baby.

Tiny life.

Laid on Dina's chest.

The feeling - God - like surging love.

The midwife handed her to Jay. The little girl. The little thing that looked so much like him.

Nothing felt like this.

Him and his little girl.

The midwife took her to give her something and test for something and it was all ok.

Worry, pride, love, hurt, the unbearable knowing of vulnerability, of something like total warmth, of peace. Of all going to be okay.

Mia. All he needed. The hours spent with her sleeping on his chest, sucking a finger, when she started to smile and wave her tiny legs and arms. These were hours of the best of the most wonder he had known.

But slowly life ticks back in.

Work.

Dina.

MOT, insurance, mortgage, bills - trips to Spain and France and games in every other city in the league.

And slowly the knowing that Mia was all he loved.

The rest was just fluff.

Including Dina.

And there was the weekend, up north, when he'd fallen on the pitch and found himself face to face with Clara in the hospital. And thought it was a waking dream, like he often had about her. But then it was real.

And they went to hotel and had sex. And then he knew why Liam had rolled his eyes at dad. And he knew what sex was and love was and what life was.

They did all they had fantasised about. Talked about.

And they talked that night - but somehow couldn't say anything that answered the questions about why this hadn't happened before and why it seemed to mean so much and why their lives had moved together and apart so many times.

Dina was nothing. He knew nothing would ever be like Clara.

But he couldn't have her and that hurt more than he could stand.

So he decided to never think about her or speak to her again.

He had Mia. All he needed.

And that was when he knew the end was near.

Jay and Clara 2019

After Billy's wake, Jay and Clara sat across from one another at a small marble effect table in one of those Italian chain restaurants in which all the menu items are the same as every other place in every town in the country. This chain had chosen to name each dish by predicating them with a region of Italy - Venetian polpetta meatballs, Sardinian sparda swordfish, Perugian ragu with spaghetti. Clara found it laughable, nearly told him so to break the ice.

But he broke the silence first.

As he spoke, she remembered his mouth on hers. How she had felt she had to touch his calves knowing they were his most valuable asset. Knowing they were what were seen in photos. She'd wanted then to look at his tattoo - but had not seen it or remembered to see it. She saw it now. ...*I lived*, it said, from the wrist a few centimetres up the right arm. Now she imagined his young body in a morgue and the tattoo poignant.

He told her he'd never been to this place. Not here in his home town. But been to one in Manchester and in Sheffield. She wanted to say she usually avoided these places, but instead smiled. I've never been to one, she said.

It was good of you to come, she said, it's a long way for someone you don't know.

Gotta give something back haven't you, he looked away from her then over her left shoulder. Then down at his fork. Straightened it. You said some emotional stuff there at the funeral Clara. You must have really cared about Billy.

Oddly, oddly then she sensed a jealousy perhaps. Or was she projecting that? Was that her shame talking, feeling? Where once, before therapy, she would have jumped to please him, to defend herself - *Oh no, barely knew him, just a kid, just have to go through the motions.* She said instead, I did care about him. He was a lost little boy and he was failed by us like I said. I feel we could have prevented it. We make too many mistakes - tar all the kids with the same brush. Don't fit, get em out.

I know you told me once, I don't owe that school anything, but I didn't do it for the school. Or for the publicity, if you are thinking that. She wasn't thinking that - this was his shame talking. Then he said, I remember everything you ever said to me. And he was looking right at her then, just as he had many times. She held those words and thought about how her body felt - thrilled, injected, alive. And she trembled - actually trembled - a strange energy exuded from her.

She sat with it. And as she noticed her tremble, it transfigured into a coldness, more of a shiver. Not of temperature but of a release, a letting go.

I do think about you, a lot, she said and made herself look in his eyes, and not avoid them as she always had. Not look away.

He sat back then. Took a huge breath and exhaled through his mouth. Me too, you have no idea.

As often happens, or so it seems, the waiter came and stood beside them at this moment, breaking the intensity. *Ready? Five more minutes.*

Yes. Five minutes thanks. Clara hadn't said it - for once, she wasn't the one making the choices, managing feelings, dealing with the expectations. For once she was going to ride this through and watch, watch her feelings and drift above it. Observe.

They both looked at the menus. The words meant nothing now. She had to go back to those moments before when she was amused by the menu, when she was taking it in to her brain. Choose something she remembered. What can you eat from here? she asked him. Ha ha, I can eat what I want. It's not like that. What do you think we have a meal plan or something? Ha! I mean we have to be careful, but the odd chicken parmigiana is okay. Clara went on to explain they were called 'parmos' where she came from - native dish of the north east. They laughed about that. He teased her about her northern vowels and she called him a soft southerner, joked about these footballers and their 'long-johns' on the pitch in the cold northern winter. She had to explain the reference to old fashioned underwear - it never used to be all 'Agent

Provocateur' when my granny was young. He looked at her chest then, and into her eyes, don't make me picture you in sexy underwear he said, or your granny!

God it was beautiful to laugh like that.

Jay remembered she was funny. He'd loved that in her lessons, how funny she could be. You can't know that about someone unless you meet them, face them, watch their body, hear the tones in their voice. That way she smiled with one side of her mouth.

When the food arrived, he wished it hadn't. There was a strangeness about eating in front of her. And the interruption was disappointing. He was laughing. It was hard to remember when he had last laughed like this, like a child laughs, without restraint.

As he ate, he thought about how he had kissed her neck. So many times he had relived their evening together, replayed it, all the details of her and how she felt. But he hadn't remembered his mouth on her neck until now.

Do you ever think about what we did together?

Yes. Of course.

What do you think about?

All of it Jay. It was lovely. How you kissed my neck. How you looked at me.

Me too. All of it.

There was silence then. He was remembering - feeling himself getting turned on.

She asked, why did you never text me after that? Ignored me.

I dunno. I couldn't. My girlfriend was around you know. And I was busy.

But that was not it - for a long time it was as if he'd had it, done it, got it, had the water from the jar, filled his beak with what he'd wanted, needed. Then over time it crept in again, that feeling of wanting more. Like a pulling. But he couldn't ask after time had passed after she had moved on. And he'd lied, promising to see her again and never seeing her. And if they met again, what was it then: a relationship, an affair, love? That was too much, not his thing, not with her, she was too much. And what if, what if she said he wasn't enough. Family first. Her family first. Respect that, respect family Jay. Family first. She was a diamond, stolen from a case, that you could never show off, never wear, never sell. Always kept but never displayed. This, whatever this was, was unknowable and unboxable and unnamable and felt too much and had fuzzy edges and couldn't be held or put in the real world. Standing by the side of the road as a sports car rushes by, beautiful for a moment, loud, desirable and then gone, a shadow and a smell and a feeling that was there that moment and then passed on forever.

Now, here, in this moment, as the edges of the tables blurred and the hunger was palpable in his fingers, but not for the food which was nothing, like a prop in a film. And as he leant his elbows on the table and put his fork down and held his own face in his hands and looked at her - this was the moment, the only alive thing, the time and the place. And he realised then that everything he'd told himself about why he couldn't contact her was a story he had created in his own head.

Everything is a story.

He was looking so intensely, intently at her. She'd watched herself when he had lied and said he'd been busy. Her loss had returned. And a fluttering of fear? Of what, of the deception, of something hidden? She saw now he'd stopped eating. So did she and she mimicked him, putting her head in her own hands like he had done and looked into his face. But just her right hand, cupping her cheek.

I'm sorry I didn't contact you. I wish I had, he said.

Me too. You hurt me.

I know. I've missed you.

I've missed you.

And now as she watched herself, she found a resistance to this solid intensity. She wanted to break it, ask a pointless question about football or his child, or whether he still saw his school mates, or something to make something distancing happen.

But instead she continued to look at him.

She didn't have to drive this; let it drive itself.

She continued looking into his eyes as she felt something rising in her chest, into her throat, like a cork moving into her mouth.

Tears.

She knew it was better to bear the sharp pain of consciousness rather than hide in the dull pain of unconsciousness. She knew bearing this pain, hard pain, made her alive.

Why are you crying?

I don't even know.

She began to laugh then - like relief or ridiculousness.

Everything shattered.

He sat back, softened. Have you ever thought about us being together? Like together, you know.

Many times. I've pictured you with me so many times….But the story I told myself was that you wouldn't want that.

Why wouldn't I? I've thought about it. But you have a family.

I'm too old for you. I'd bore you.

What? Is that what you think? I'd fuckin bore you. My life is boring. I'm not interesting at all.

He really meant that, maybe she'd think he was trying to get a compliment, for her to contradict him. But he had thought about it and he did think he'd bore her. And anyway she was better than him, settled, happy.

He felt angry now. Why did she think she was boring? That was…not possible…another story.

You're not boring Clara. You are amazing. Interesting. Intriguing, is that the word…Miss?

Ha! Miss…yes that's the word. Thank you Jay.

And you are fucking hot. My brother said once to me, you can't choose who you happen to like. I mean that's just how life is.

You are right. You can't choose. It just keeps pulling you back in.

That's it. That's exactly like it is.

As he said that he felt the buzz, the rush, the tremble he'd known with her before.

His phone was moving in his pocket. Ringing. He took it out, saw the screen. His mum. Knew he couldn't leave his daughter with her any longer – it was about that time of the evening when his mother would start to fall, to sleep, to not function.

Look Clara, I'm sorry. This isn't an excuse but I've got to get my daughter from my mum. I have to go pretty soon.

It's ok. I know how it is. Guess I'd better get back too.

Jay felt the weight of it then. Fuck, he said, life is so much harder when you have kids. It's not simple anymore.

I don't know it if ever was Jay.

God, it's been amazing to see you.

You too.

Clara was sad. So sad. And the numbness had started to move in. This is how we manage those long known feelings - the hole, the want, the loss, the little girl left crying that was still right there in her. As they stood by his car, they hugged, and it was long and felt deeply and had all the melding and blending and dissolving of bodies and bones that embraces should have. And they kissed right there in the car park. It was charged with risk. But they knew it and also knew they'd care later, but not now.

I'm sorry I have to love you and leave you.

Me too Jay.

He got in the car, she turned away. He was gone.

Jay felt fucking awful on the long drive back. His little girl slept in the back, all the way, in the dark. He'd found her asleep fully dressed on the sofa, mum in bed, no one else to be found in the house. He couldn't let her have the life he had had. He had to give her a happy home with money. Money was what would make it different. But his soul jabbed him - it's more than that, it told him. He wished he'd told Clara, I love you. But what would that achieve? And anyway, she'd drifted away at the end. She could have said it. She didn't.

Clara got home. The lights were out. Her husband had closed the study door, his light still on in there. Her son was asleep. She felt like she was the only human on the planet - an end of days, an apocalypse, the sole survivor. What was the fucking point in that? Jay had said something like, I love you. Why hadn't she replied - said it too? But he was the one who'd ended it, gone back to some blonde girlfriend no doubt, bored with her company. Her soul said, no it's not that - there was all the feeling and not the words to say it.

And there they were, back in the place where everything was possible, but there was not enough courage to step into something different and listen to that part of them that was holding on to each other and screaming to be heard.
Above the should, should, should not.

Jay 2019

There are a lot of matches around Christmas mum, you know that. I can't get home. Sorry. I can see Liam another time mum. Family first, I know mum, but I haven't got time. Last year was different mum. I had more days in between games. I'll FaceTime you Christmas day.

He didn't want to go home.

Liam wouldn't go if he wasn't going to be there as his ally.

Dad wouldn't care, as long as his son was a top-notch on-the-TV footballer. Nothing else mattered.

Jay didn't want to do much these days. He trained, sometimes played, spent a lot of time on the bench. Watching his colleagues was like watching football on TV. Of course he could get totally into it, enjoy it even, but unlike watching on tv, he knew he should be on the pitch. Could do a better job than some of them. You never said that sort of thing, but he felt it.

When he wasn't playing or training, he watched sport, any sport. Gambled. Didn't matter. He had money to throw away if he wanted to. Sometimes he won - mostly on the horses.

Turned twenty-six. Felt like he should buy a house. He had been looking. Big places - didn't matter where if it was near an airport, he could fly back for days off, whatever. Next year he could do Christmas, have it catered, if he didn't have a girlfriend to cook for his family by then.

A big house, maybe with a pool, a new car and a girlfriend. That would make him happy. And an ankle that didn't keep giving way on him. Not much he could do about that.

He'd been to look at a place not long ago. A few weeks after that dinner with Clara. It was not far from home, in a country village, twenty minutes drive from the airport. It was gated. Had one of those buzzer entry boxes on a gate post. Jay had liked that touch. The house was not visible from the road, surrounded by a high manicured box hedge. It had a long drive and a half moon shaped gravel patch outside the front door, on which was parked a car just like his own, even in the same shade of petrol blue.

He was shown around the house, with the archway-like stone entrance, the underground cinema room, the huge open plan living room and kitchen, which even had a boiling water tap. The house had tennis courts and planning permission for a pool in one of the out buildings.

Jay was acting, acting entitled. He deserved this place. Any place like this.

But some part of him felt not good enough.

He kept fantasising Clara there, looking with him. She'd look good here. It had a playroom which was the only room not tidied - the table in there had been used for crafts, covered in paint splatters and dried glue. Boxes of torn paper and felt were stacked against the walls. Her son would like it here. His little girl would like it here. He'd build a pool for them.

But driving away, he was empty.

He didn't want to come back here again. Even the familiar road signs made his chest hurt. This wasn't the place to live.

He flew back north through the drizzle and back in his flat, whilst he glared unseeing out of the window and over the river, he called for a pizza. Checked Facebook while he waited - trawled through the selfies and pouts and tattoos and foreign holidays and couples on beaches and couples on trains and couples with babies.

He called Dina: *Alright, how's Mia? Yeah Monday I know. What can't I check in when I ain't with her? Upset her? What you on about? Fuck off Dina - I just wanna see how she is. Is your bloke there or summink? Just put her on hey?…Mia baby, it's daddy. I love you. Be a good girl for mummy. I'm gonna see you Monday baby. Bye baby….Yeah alright. See ya.*

Ended the call.

He lifted the phone. Smoothed his hair to the right. Made sure the designer couch was in the corner of the shot. Lifted his hand a fraction higher. Took a selfie. Scrolled through the filters. Black and white. #daysoff #COYB #lovinlife and posted it on Instagram.

Later, after the pizza, during an hour or two, or more, watching athletics, he checked his phone. The likes rolled in. The comments. He felt good.

But once the likes slowed to a trickle he became vapid, vacant, empty.

That night he checked his Messenger. Still: 'you cannot reply to this conversation'. Tried to friend her on Instagram, Snapchat, Twitter @CHorton27 - she didn't accept his request.
And that is how easy it is to erase someone from your life - grief is grief regardless of the loss.
It hurt.
He stayed up that night, bet on the athletics, lost. Slept. Dosed. Felt a burning fear that everything would always feel this way.
He only just made it to training the next day. He was tired. Exhausted. The green glare of the astro-turf hurt his eyes. The drills felt hard, knocked a cone at one point, thought to himself 'power up'. He couldn't do it.

You ain't on good form Jay. You ill?

No coach. I'm alright. Dunno what's wrong.

You eating right? Sleeping? Never seen you like this mate.

Dunno. Just not on form coach.

Later that day, he sat alone in the changing room, elbows on his knees, head in his hands. He just felt shit, like it all meant nothing. Like it was all so pointless. Like it was too hard, too much. He looked at his boots, locked in around his feet - his feet were the only bit of him that were worth anything.

Some words he had heard once came back to him: 'Must be strange though to think you are a commodity. Something to be bought and sold until you are not good enough anymore.'

The coach came in. Stood right in front of him. Jay lifted his eyes. Coach sat down next to him on the bench, silent. For a while they both looked at the floor.

Jay, you're a good player. You know that. You are still growing - we all are. But I'm worried about you mate. Look I really think you should see someone, like a therapist, just someone to talk to who's not gonna judge, to get you back on track. We have people here, professionals, or you can choose your own. The sport's changing mate, loads of players do it. I can't tell you what to do, but maybe it would help. I've made an appointment with the nutritionist for you, just to check in, you know.

Jay was silent.

I'm not gonna play you this weekend. I've told the gaffer. You should get yourself off somewhere. Visit family maybe, go see your brother. Take some time out Jay.

Are you sacking me?

No Jay. Just asking you to take a break mate. That's all.

The coach held Jay's wrist for a moment. Then said, *You're gonna be alright.*

When he left, Jay felt his own nails digging into his palms. He stood, suddenly, turned, punched the wall behind him. *Fuck!* Screamed it. He paced around the changing room, leaning one or twice against the walls, pushing them. His breath came with difficulty. He gathered his stuff, throwing it into his bag. Grappled in the side pocket for his car keys. Left the building slamming every door behind him. *Fuck this!* he shouted in the car park.

He drove. At first he didn't know where to. Maybe he intended to go home, back to the flat, but then he decided he would go to Liam, he would. So he signaled left at the roundabout that took him out of the city, onto the motorway and towards Sheffield.

Liam was out when Jay arrived at the house he shared with his girlfriend. She was out too. It was a small, terraced house with dark stone walls and a quaint charm like something from a film about the Victorians. He sat on the step and waited. People walked by, not many, but a few. One guy stopped, looked, took in the training kit Jay was still wearing and spat at his feet. But all the anger was gone from Jay; he felt nothing. Felt he deserved it.

Liam's bike sped around the end of the street and into view. He slowed, visibly, removed his headphones - by now it was getting dark and he peered to see who the shape was on his door step. *What the fuck are you doing here Jay?* He hugged him as Jay rose, stiff in his body, tired -

so tired - and cold. *Come in and get off this street before someone beats you up. In that top! You are brave around here.*

Didn't even think about it bruv. I need to talk, I think.

Liam made them both a cup of tea and Jay sat on the second-hand leather sofa which seemed to swallow him, embrace him. He pulled the throw over himself, lay down, closed his eyes. He tried to think about what he had come here to say - didn't even know.

When Liam came back in, he sat opposite on the matching leather chair. He watched Jay sip the tea, too hot, watched him cradle it in his hands. Liam stood, and for some time rummaged around lighting a fire. Jay watched, totally numb, just observing the flames as they began to take hold of the kindling and then the coal. Liam sat again in the chair and waited for Jay to speak. Someone would break the silence.

Don't even know why I came here. Just needed to get away. They ain't playing me Saturday.

Liam waited in silence.

I feel shit Liam. Really fucking shit. And I don't even know why. I feel like I just wanna go to bed and not get up. But I can't can I? My life don't work like that.

Doesn't it? Why not? Liam was gentle - not accusing.

Cos I gotta play. Gotta be seen. Can't just vanish. My career will be over.

Who is telling you that?

Jay almost said 'everyone,' but then he knew the answer. It wasn't everyone.

Dunno, dad I guess. The gaffer. The fans. Me....myself....I would feel like I was a loser, you know, a failure.

People sometimes feel bad Jay. They feel ill, or depressed. It's okay to feel that way. Perhaps you need to forget what other people think and start looking after yourself.

Yeah I'm trying mate. I wanna buy a house, maybe get a new car.

Liam sat again in silence. Jay got out his phone, started searching for something.

Here, look at this place. It's in somewhere called Bramfield, like not far from here. Fucking massive. Look.

Liam didn't look. Instead he asked, *do those things make you happy? The car, the swanky flat, the expensive trainers.*

Yeah.

But you have them, and you are not happy. Well that is you caring what other people think. As long as you are thinking about the next big purchase...the next match... the fame, I dunno Jay, it just feels like you...you will always be sort of fighting with yourself.

But it's my job mate.

No - playing football is your job, because you love it don't ya and you are good at it and you enjoy it. The rest is fluff and air. That's all it is – well that's what I think.

For a while Jay stared into the flames. He felt his body melting, no sensation, no hurt in his chest. All he felt was the tea sliding down his throat, almost felt it gliding into his stomach.

Feels good here bruv. Cosy you know, safe. You are happy. How'd you do it?

I'm not always happy, but when I'm not I just say to myself, 'I'm unhappy right now and that's ok, it's just how I feel'. Sometimes there's a reason, sometimes not.

Jay's mind went back to when Liam had been broken, so unhappy, wailing in pain on the floor, busted arm – Jay had wheeled him on his bike to hospital, holding him on the seat like a little child whilst he walked along steadying the frame.

Look Jay, I had to grow up with Dad hitting me and telling me I was a failure. I've had to deal with that…I have had to learn that what others say and do isn't under my control and that they do it because they are hurt. Someone hurt them. I have had to learn, and like really learn, that what makes happiness is being ok with yourself, you know like knowing you are a good person. Sometimes mate, seriously, I have to go and say nice things to myself, out loud.

They both laughed at this.

I know, I know…but that's how I manage. That's how I have found some relief from all the pain have had. Look, I can't tell you what to do but all I can say is, give yourself a break. I mean an actual break and a break, like stop beating yourself up.

Tiredness overtook Jay. He asked if he could stay the night, if Alison didn't mind. And when she came home she embraced him warmly, so much so that he nearly cried. Liam cooked a stew and as Jay sat around their table in the tiny kitchen, he was laughing and joking with them both. The stew was warming, like it was building him again. And after, he felt like he just wanted to sleep. He undressed and got under the covers in his boxers, not even caring he'd been in them since dawn. As he began to drift off, he looked over to the disused fireplace in the bedroom which Alison had jigsawed some books into to fill the gap. He spotted a title, *The Great Gatsby*. He knew it from somewhere and began to trawl his memory for it as he fell asleep.

When he woke, for a few seconds he felt blissful, innocent. Then the memory of all that had happened and all he had felt came tumbling back upon him. In that moment, the hole returned to his chest. He got up, showered, dressed and went downstairs. It was early. He made some tea, had some toast, standing in the kitchen.

He went to get his things and, just as he was leaving the room, grabbed the book from the fireplace. The others fell out of place. He nearly left them on the floor but knelt to re-stack them, best he could.

Alison came in behind him, in her pyjamas covered with a bear hooded fleece. She helped him stack the last few books. *Sorry*, he said.

That's fine. It was only supposed to be a temporary measure. I guess we should get a book shelf. Just never get round to it.

I think it looks good like that. Different ain't it? Can I borrow this one?

Sure. Haven't you read it?

No I don't really read to be honest. But I remembered the title of this one. Not sure where from.

Maybe because it was a film.

No, somewhere else. Is it good?

Yes. A classic. It's about a man pretending to be someone he isn't in a world of money and excess, basically to get the girl he loves. He's called Jay actually.

I'll give it a go - thanks.

He hugged Alison at the door, told her not to wake Liam and that he'd see them soon.

Got in his car, tossed the book onto the back seat and sped off.

Clara 2019

Clara sat in the chair opposite her therapist, a blanket over her knees. She held a cup of mint tea in her hands, feeling the warmth of it through her palms.

He tried to contact me yesterday. I saw he'd sent me a request on Twitter. I ignored it.

And how did that feel?

I wanted to accept him. I wanted to talk to him again. But I know it will make me feel worse. I know it's a fantasy, an avoidance, a way of not connecting with what's going on in my life.

And what is going on in your life Clara?

Clara observed the wall go up. The discomfort rising. The desire to stop this conversation; redirect it. But instead, she sat, in silence, waiting for the truth to come.

I'm unhappy. I'm sad. I'm angry. I don't know who I am. I don't feel joy, ever. I go to work where I feel like I'm disliked and nothing like myself. I mean, I don't know who that is, but it is not that hard-hearted bitch I take to work with me every day. I'm tired and pissed off at home. You know, I have nothing of myself left. Nothing.

And Jay gave you a bit of yourself back. Reminded you of how it feels to be noticed and loved.

Yes.

And so it is brave to let that go.

Clara felt vulnerable, scared. It is hard to say that, to say, there is nothing of me left. She felt the rising thickness driving up through her chest. And she cried, on and on she cried. When her therapist said, *there's some tissues there*, she was surprised to find herself still in the room, in the chair, and still whole and not dissolved, because that was how she saw herself now. Dissolved.

What made you cry Clara, do you think?

I am nothing. I think I feel relieved I said that. And then, you said a kind thing to me, called me brave. I think that made me cry.

You haven't had a lot of kindness in your life. You've had a lot of loss. It's not surprising you feel this way. Give yourself a break Clara. Be kind to yourself.

I know. You have told me to and I'm trying. It just feels so strange, talking to myself and saying kind things.

Because you don't believe them? Because you don't feel worthy of them?

Yes. I think so.

For a while they sat in silence. Clara felt her breath - short and shallow.

Our time is up for today. This has been a tough session. You are doing well Clara. Go for a long walk, if you can, and look around you. Give yourself time to process what you have experienced today.

The next day was Friday. Her husband had got up and gone out to work early - she had felt him get up, and leave, heard the front door close. When she woke, she felt for her phone by the bed. Texted the Head and his PA, *Not coming in today. I'm unwell.* Emailed a cover lesson for Year 7 to the Head of English.

Then, for the first time, ever, she took her Harry to school at normal school time, dropping him in his classroom. She had never seen his teacher before, had missed parents' evenings and every school event. Never seen a Nativity or a prize giving assembly. Harry showed her off to his friends, to the teaching assistant, and she looked around at those women she had always called 'gate mums', wondering how the hell they managed to be there at 8.40 every morning. Now she saw, she resented their lives, whatever they were. A dad of a friend of Harry's, who she thought was called Gareth, walked back across the playground with her.

We don't usually see you here? Non-pupil day at yours is it?

Just giving myself a day off.

Bloody well deserved. I don't know how you do it.

She didn't even know what he did for a living, and couldn't ask there and then. Sounded accusing in her head, 'what do you do then?' and so she smiled and agreed and said it was hard work.

Something in Gareth's gait as he walked away reminded her for a moment of her old friend James Moles. He'd been so much fun. Times were better then, when she could go out and stay out with friends. When she could flirt and banter and know it meant nothing. Moles had moved to Scotland to become a part time Forest Schools teacher – she never heard from him after that, except for the odd Facebook comment. Recently nothing at all. 'Off grid' they said about him.

She had become to envy him for that; unrestrained and free.

She drove out to a village not far from her house. It was where her mother was born. She knew a footpath she'd once been shown on a map, by her dad. The path went from the village to the coast and along the sea wall before turning back in towards the road. And as the winter sun began to break through the mist lying on the fields, she took the path and walked out towards the sea. To her right lay the marshy inlets thick with mud and samphire. To her left, the dike cut deeply into the landscape and the bulrushes reached high from the mad-made river that ran alongside the path.

At the sea wall, the North Sea stretching endless in front of her, Clara stopped. She closed her eyes. Felt her body. She felt desperately lonely.

But then, she began to hear the waves and the sea birds. She began to smell the sea and to feel the coldness at the ends of her fingers and her knees and her toes and on her cheeks. She saw the light as it lit up the capillaries in her eyelids, the red lines dancing through the skin. And for those few moments, she felt relief. Pain ebbed away and something like joy, like freedom came to her.

On the walk back, Clara passed through a field of something at first undefinable. She stopped and looked at the vegetable growing low to the ground. Tall stalks stood from the soil, and she saw they were brussel sprouts growing there. She thought of Christmas and how really most people must eat sprouts only on Christmas Day. Then her memory reminded her of a story her grandmother had told her about losing seven babies, always in a sprout field, always in winter, always with the frost on the ground and numb, frozen fingers. Her grandmother had worked in the fields when her mother and aunt were young - picking vegetables and fruit all year round. Before mechanisation and immigration did the job. And through those tough winters, bent low, seven babies died inside her. Seven.

And Clara considered that her mother had survived, born after the seven babies. And how much hurt her mother had brought her. And how Clara had fallen into being treated that same way again and again. How she went to work and felt that hurt, and saw that same hurt in the kids she taught.

And she knew she couldn't keep putting herself through this. Who had decided she had to be this machine? She had relinquished her humanity, her instinct, her soul, her feeling in the drive to not be like her mother. Maybe more, to be the perfect picture of womanhood she saw everywhere - every Facebook post and every 'successful' woman in every broadsheet article. And yet there she was, being like her mother - cold, broken, hurt, desperate, seeking control, wanting to be loved.

Clara pictured her mother as a woman of her own age, with a child of six or seven, in an age of beauty shows, and morning fitness on TV, and diet books, and Diana and Dynasty and a husband who spent all day at a typewriter, attending book launches and dining with executives and beautiful young writers. She knew then, her mother, like her, had lost everything of herself in the pursuit of being the perfect picture of womanhood.

Well Clara needed to take it back. Whatever it took.

Almost back to the car, Clara ran her hand along the hedgerow. A holly bush caught her eye, so vibrant both in its greens and reds. Holly grows in the darkest months, berries form against the coldest winds, withstanding snow and frost: Berried red life, glistening waxed leaves, edges with barbs. No one gets past. Reminds us of life in the season of death.

She tore off a branch and took it home - to remember.

Christmas came. They call it a break but for Clara it had always been anything but that. The hectic days of work are replaced by the hectic days of shopping, wrapping, cooking, hosting and tolerating.

This year was different.

She had told her husband: *We aren't having family this year, not even Dad. You are cooking Christmas dinner - like you did when we were first together. I'll do the clearing up. And we are going to play with Harry, really play with him and his Lego and puzzles and robots and draw and paint and cut up all the Christmas cards to make decorations for the tree. And go for a really long walk, down to the sea.*

He was surprised. And then he did something she couldn't remember him doing for many months, maybe longer; he hugged her. And said 'okay'.

And then, on the evening of Christmas Day, when Harry was in bed and they sat trawling Netflix for something they could both watch, she said: *You know what, things have been pretty shit for me, and for us for so long that it feels like normal. But it's not normal. Or I don't want it to be. I have had enough. I'm going to make some big changes, I don't even know what they are going to be. But I don't want to feel like this. So, if you agree, let's start with this - one night, every week, no phones, no work and we just sit together, you and me, and we watch a film or play a game or read books together or whatever. Just be. You know?*

He said he had a lot of work and they didn't share the same taste in films and he didn't have a book to read at the moment.

But an hour later, he said they could try. At least try.

On Boxing Day, he turned on the football show he watched at the weekend. All the big clubs, with their badges and colours and symbols. The big names running around on the TV in the corner of her own living room. Clara asked him to turn it off.

Sometimes, when your mind is clear and you are beginning to look at what is around you, at a time when you are ready, an answer comes. It just lands in front of you, ready for you to receive it. At least, that is what Clara thought as she opened her emails on the first day back. Her inbox had a message in it entitled, 'Consultancy?' It was from an ex-colleague of hers who now worked at a private school. It read: *Hi Clara. I hope you don't mind me contacting you at work. I know it is a bit cheeky but I have a proposal for you. A friend of mine has set up a teaching consultancy firm and is looking for someone to run sessions on 'OFSTED ready'. I thought of you. I wonder if school might release you for a couple of days a week. It pays well, I can assure you! Thinking about it myself in fact. Anyway, I'll leave it with you. If you are interested, contact my friend at….*

And suddenly that was it. She knew what she would do. Two days a week, consultancy, and she didn't even care if it 'paid well'. She just knew it was going to be the start of this new way, this new path. It all fell away from her, the heaviness of years and years. The fizzing returned to her, the life, the energy - something of herself. That night she stayed late, drafting her resignation.

The following day, she was sitting at her desk, about to pick up the phone to call the Head and ask him if they could meet, when a student arrived carrying a yellow slip of paper. Emergency cover lesson.

She didn't look at the details to begin with, just felt the usual anger and slight trepidation of having to step into a class that wasn't hers. And the time it would take from her day, already over-scheduled.

Then she saw the room number: EB12. It had been years since she had stepped into that room.

She noticed it was laid out differently. Tables in a horseshoe - never worked in her opinion. Walls redecorated of course. But it smelled the same. And God how evocative that smell was. The Year 10s sat in silence, doing a test. Clara scanned the room - she imagined herself there as a much younger woman; how different she was then, how much more real, more raw, more human, even with the kids.

And of course she thought of Jay. Felt him there through the thin veil that existed between them. Sometimes she thought she could feel him thinking about her. She knew she had hurt him; she could feel it intensely, as if he stood next to her. Clara had avoided this room for so long because she knew she would feel as she did right now, such depth of grief, such regret, and the edges of feelings she had no name for.

Clara drifted through the hour, not even logging on, not taking the register, not once engaging with anything outside of her reminisces and consciousness of her body and the watching, watching she was doing of herself. And the memories which tore at her.

But within that was a wistful knowing - that it all was, and that it all happened, and that now it was all gone.

As she began to leave the room, still used for English as it had been in her time, she saw on the back of the door a quote from F. Scott Fitzgerald: "Love isn't like it is in the books." The title underneath made her smile, *Emotional Bankruptcy*.

Certainly true, she said out loud, into the empty classroom. And she shut the classroom door.

Printed in Great Britain
by Amazon